FROM MY WINDOW

BY

MARY LEE PECK, Ph.D.

Reading Research Institute

Westerville, Ohio

ISBN-13: 978-1-931365-09-3

ISBN 10: 1-931365-09-1

From My Window

Website: http://readingresearchinsitute.org

Printed in U.S.A.

Other Fiction Books By The Author

Raven's Call

Raven's Son

Raven's Return (coming in 2015)

The Mansion

Breakfast with Friends

Non-Fiction Books By The Author

The Family Bitch

A Balanced Approach to Reading
Instruction

FROM MY WINDOW

By
MARY LEE PECK

MARY LEE PECK

CHAPTER 1

"Excuse me," said Lauren Allen as she approached the elderly couple comfortably situated in their seats on the gigantic plane. "I'm sorry, but my seat is next to you by the window."

"It's all right, dear," replied the elderly woman. She immediately turned toward her scowling husband and nudged him to get him to move out of the way.

Lauren heard his exasperated sigh as he begrudgingly unfastened the extended seat belt from around his large, round girth and heaved himself into the narrow aisle. She apologized again and quickly slid into the seat next to the window. Struggling to shove her large bag under the seat in front of her, she bumped against the serving tray and loosened the latch holding it back. It dropped onto the top of her head. "Ouch," she muttered as she gave her bag another determined shove.

The woman beside her quickly reached over to lift the tray off her head. "Are you okay?" she asked with concern. "They certainly don't give us much wiggle room in these flying sardine cans, do they?"

"No, they don't," muttered Lauren. "Thank you for rescuing me from the tray." She forced herself to smile into the woman's kind, blue eyes and hoped that her dark sunglasses hid from view her bloodshot, swollen ones.

Finally situated in her seat, she rolled up her woolen scarf to use as a pillow against the cold, hard window.

Immediately, the tears she had tried to hold back streamed down her cheeks. Reaching in her pocket, she pulled out the small package of tissues she had stuffed in there earlier and dabbed at the flowing tears. Stop it. Tears are not going to change anything, for heaven's sake. It's over—end of story—new book, first chapter. Oh my god, I am fated to end up alone and miserable.

She reached for a second tissue as another flood of tears soaked her face. No. I won't let that happen. I don't believe in fate. I am the master of my destiny. I have a career. It will get me through this and any other misfortune that life throws my way. Love is overrated anyway. It's nothing but hormones gone wild. I may end up alone, but I refuse to be miserable.

Shifting uncomfortably in her seat, she drew in a deep breath and tried to focus her attention on the activity outside the window. The snow swirled in circles around the parka-clad workers on the tarmac. Several of them huddled closely together as they donned their bright orange vests with the glow-in-the-dark, chartreuse stripes. One of the men handed the others large wands capped with an orange, cone-shaped light that they would use to communicate with the pilots.

Signals, it's all about reading and understanding the signals. Why couldn't I have read the signals coming from Derrick? There must have been early signals that I either ignored or simply missed.

A long train of carts pulled by a small utility truck covered with dingy, white vinyl curtains and a plastic window for the driver caught her attention as it made its way toward the plane. It was stacked high with luggage and came to a jerky stop beneath her window. She watched as one of the suitcases tumbled onto the dirty, slush-covered ground. The driver leaped off the tractor and nonchalantly tossed the snow-covered suitcase onto

8

the conveyer belt that carried it up into the belly of the plane. Lauren shook her head. *I hope that bag is waterproof.*

She shifted around in her seat and stared up at the observation deck above the terminal. Through the swirling snow, she surveyed the people huddled close to the huge, floor-to-ceiling windows that overlooked the tarmac. A few of them were happily waving to someone on the plane; others simply were staring blankly out the window. One young woman was holding up a sign with the words, *I love you. Be safe,* hand-written in huge letters. She was frantically waving and blowing tearful kisses to someone on the plane. Standing next to her, an older man was holding a small child who was inconsolably crying and stretching out both of her tiny arms toward the plane. Lauren watched as the young child pounded against the window and pushed her face up against the cold glass causing the glass to fog up and her face to look strangely distorted. Tears were streaming down the cheeks of the man holding the child as he unsuccessfully tried to console her.

The young woman finally turned to the child and took her into her arms, hugged her tightly against her, and gently patted her on the back as she slowly swayed back and forth. The older man then took the sign and held it up as he offered a salute to the traveler. Lauren recalled seeing a young man in a military uniform board the plane ahead of her. She felt certain that he was the target of the stressful good bye. She reached for another tissue and dabbed at her eyes. *At least these tears are not self-pitying ones.*

A pushback tractor whipped into the gate area, and the driver carefully positioned it in front of the plane. Several of the ground-workers rushed to attach a long, tow bar to the nose of the plane, and one of them signaled to the pilot that they were ready for the pushback process to begin. On cue, the stewardess announced that the doors were closed and that they were backing away from the gate.

"This is it," she mumbled. As the plane was slowly pushed backward, she tried to decipher the signals from the ground crew as they systematically waved their orange wands to direct their departure. As the plane rolled away from the gate, she quickly glanced up again at the window where the distraught family had been standing. The older man had his arms wrapped around the mother and the child as he helped to lead them away from the giant window—more tears, another tissue.

Once they had cleared the gate, the pushback tractor was somehow automatically disconnected, and the plane pulled away from it under its own power. She glanced once more through the frosty window at the blowing snow enveloping the familiar airport. "Goodbye New York, good bye memories—good and bad," she whispered quietly.

The friendly voice of the stewardess announced that a long line of planes waiting their turn on the runway was causing a delay of their departure and that they should remain seated, turn off all electronics, ensure that their seatbelts were fastened, their seats upright, and their bags securely stored under the seat in front of them. Lauren sighed and dabbed at the stream of tears once more cascading down her cheeks.

After a twenty-minute delay, with Lauren constantly sopping up stinging tears and accumulating a pile of used tissues on her lap, it was finally their turn to take off. The plane zoomed down the long stretch of concrete until it smoothly lifted from the ground. She watched the blur of buildings and trees shrink and finally disappear as the plane soared higher and higher, leaving behind the snowy, gray day and breaking through the clouds into the bright sunshine that was hidden from the New Yorkers below.

The pressure from the g-forces pushing her back against the seat intensified the tremendous heaviness she had been feeling in her chest since Derrick had made his startling announcement. She squeezed her eyes shut as tightly as she could and tried to make the picture disappear from her mind of Derrick's cold, unapologetic face when he arrived empty handed at her apartment this morning.

An uncontrollable sob caused her whole body to shake as the tears once again gushed from her eyes. She reached for another tissue, but the packet was empty. "Oh great," she moaned as she wiped the tears away with her hand.

"Do you want to talk about it?" asked the elderly woman next to her as she handed Lauren another pack of tissues. "I'm a good listener, and it's a long flight to San Diego."

"I, I'm sorry," sobbed Lauren, haplessly tossing her hands into the air. "I can't seem to control the crying. I apologize, but I don't need to spoil your trip with my trivial life story."

"No life story is trivial," soothed the woman gently patting Lauren's tear-soaked hand. "I don't want to pry, but sometimes it helps to talk to a stranger who has no vested interest in whatever it is that seems to be breaking your heart. If and when you're ready, I'll be glad to listen."

Lauren sucked in a deep breath. Grateful to have someone to talk to, she began tearfully telling the woman about Derrick. After hours of pouring her heart out as they sailed across the country above the clouds, she ended with, "I had no clue. I feel like such an idiot."

The woman smiled and squeezed Lauren's trembling hand. "You can't control how others treat you, and you can't change what has already happened, but what you can do is to control what happens next. You're young and have the possibility of wonderful things ahead of you. Do me a favor. When you get to California, go and sit by the ocean just as the sun is setting. Let the vastness of the ocean and the beauty of the sunset help you find perspective. The ocean is a great healer. You'll see."

CHAPTER 2

After fumbling to find the right key to her new condo, Lauren finally managed to open the door. It was dark, and she was exhausted from her emotional turmoil, the long flight, and the typical hassles associated with claiming luggage and finding a taxi in a crowded airport.

After several moments of running her hand along the smooth surface of the entranceway wall, she finally located the light switch and flipped it on. Nothing happened. "Of course," she moaned. "No light bulbs. You'd think they could have at least left one bulb at the rate I am paying to lease this place."

Reaching into her jacket pocket, she pulled out her iPhone and switched on the flashlight app. Through the stream of light from the phone, she could see the moving company's boxes stacked and scattered around the room. A brief moment of gratitude that at least her things had arrived as promised flashed through her otherwise thoroughly depressed mind.

Carefully dragging her small suitcase behind her, she made her way to the familiar couch that had been dropped in the middle of the living room. She pulled off the plastic wrap covering it and plopped down without even taking off her coat. Curling up in a fetal position, she hugged herself tightly and cried herself into fitful sleep.

Daylight gradually streamed in through the uncovered windows of her condo, and Lauren slowly began to awaken. She rubbed her eyes and tried to adjust to the light. Without lifting her head, she glanced around the

13

room at the boxes and the scattered furniture. She immediately unwrapped her wool scarf from around her neck and put it over her eyes to block out the sun and the reality of her disheveled life.

Arriving at the condo should have been exciting—a moment that was to have been joyously shared with Derrick. He had flown out with her to California when she interviewed for the position as the Head Curator at the Museum, and after checking out the condo together, they had agreed that it was a perfect place for him to continue his writing career. When she was offered the job, he had encouraged her to accept it. It wasn't until yesterday morning that she learned that he never had any intentions of moving to California with her. His cold, insensitive words pounded in her head.

'Lauren, I don't love you; in fact, I don't think I've ever really loved you. You're an intelligent, beautiful woman, but you are not the person that I want to spend my life with. I wish you well in California,' he had said, and then he had calmly walked out of her apartment and out of her life.

She had met Derrick five years ago when she had first arrived in New York. She had fled to New York to start a new life after a failed romance with her college sweetheart who ran off with her supposed, best friend. Looking for another romantic relationship in New York was the furthest thing from her mind, but then she met Derrick. At forty, he was ten years older than she was and appeared so much more sophisticated and worldly than any of the other men she knew. He was tall and handsome with dark hair that had a light hint of gray at his temples. He was a freelance writer who had enjoyed some success with published articles in the *New Yorker.*

He frequented the museum where she was an associate curator, and he always requested to be part of her

14

lectures and tours. For more than a year, they were just casual acquaintances until he finally asked her out. After that first date, they had been exclusively dating for three and a half years, and she had felt that she finally had found someone who would be her lifetime partner.

How could I have been so blind, not once but twice, she wondered as she flipped over to bury her face in the back of the couch? "That sun is relentless," she groaned.

She tried to recall if Derrick had given her any indication that he wasn't serious about their relationship. No. He told me he loved me every day. True, he had never asked me to move in with him, but I was okay with that because I knew that he needed his solitude for his writing. How could he just wake up yesterday morning and decide that he no longer loved me or that he never did? How could he have been so cruel as to lead me on for three and a half years—never dating anyone else, always there for me, and only pretending to love me?

Completely exasperated and bewildered, she angrily pounded the back of the couch with her fists. Flipping back over, the rays of the bright sun burned through her closed eyes. "Oh, all right. You win," she shouted to the sun as she got up and walked over to the window. "The first thing I buy is a set of blinds to shut you out."

She unlocked the sliding glass door and shoved it along the track to open it. A fresh breeze instantly filled the room, and she stepped out onto the small verandah. The warm surface of the balcony floor felt good on her feet, and the sun felt hot on her face. She drew in a deep breath. "This most certainly beats the gray days, unrelenting snow, and polluted arctic air of New York," she said.

She tilted her face upward and let the sun shine down on her tear-stained cheeks. Finally, opening her eyes she glanced down at her watch. "Ten o'clock in New York; seven o'clock here." She immediately reset her watch. "There," she said. "No more comparisons. No looking back and no more relationships. I've been burned twice. Fooled once, shame on him. Fooled twice, shame on me."

She glanced quickly over at the verandah of the condo next to hers. She was certain that she had heard a woman's sarcastic chuckle coming from that direction, but there was no one there. "Hmm, that's strange," she said.

She shook her head and turned her attention toward the small beach just to the north of her condo. She was amazed to see a group of wetsuit clad swimmers stepping into the ocean. Wow! They must be dedicated, or nuts she marveled as she watched the swimmers make their way slowly over the gentle rolling waves. "That water has to be cold."

Turning her gaze toward the horizon, she could see nothing but water meeting sky. "So vast, so mysterious," she muttered. "It is humbling and healing, just as my airplane friend had said." She inhaled deeply and felt a tiny bit of her sadness slowly slipping away.

"Good morning," called a frail, elderly woman who was slowly walking her equally elderly English bulldog along the long ocean overlook that passed in front of her condo. "Beautiful day isn't it? Makes you glad to be alive."

Lauren smiled down at her from her verandah and waved as the woman shuffled on up the street, stopping occasionally to encourage her lagging dog to catch up.

I wonder if she's ever had a broken heart, Lauren mused. Probably. Hasn't everyone? But she's still glad to be alive and looks happy enough. She chuckled as the woman leaned down and finally picked up the worn out dog, obviously scolding him for his unwillingness to continue their journey.

She was about to go back inside when she noticed an odd-looking tricycle coming around the corner and creeping unhurriedly down the street. Lying back against a black leather seat, an older man slowly pedaled the strange-looking vehicle. He casually pushed against the large pedals that turned the oversized wheels in steady, leisurely revolutions making it appear to Lauren that she was watching a slow motion movie. The trike reminded her of an old racing roadster without the hood or body. Its long, needle nose stuck out ahead of a slanted, padded, single seat and large, elevated handlebars. The pedals were near the front of the vehicle allowing the rider to practically lie down as he pedaled. He wore goggles and a leather coat and hat. The hat had lamb's wool-lined earmuffs that loosely covered his ears. A thin, leather strap dangled from the ear muffs and rested on the collar of his jacket. Lauren smiled and wondered if he had once been a pilot or perhaps a racecar driver.

As she watched, the man looked up and saluted her. Definitely, a pilot, she decided as she waved back at him.

Finally tearing herself away from the magnificent view, she turned to face the disorganized mass of boxes and cluttered furniture that awaited her inside the condo. "Okay, I can do this," she declared. She grabbed the box labeled *Bathroom* and headed down the hallway. She drew in a long, deep breath and felt her confidence slowly start to return. "First, a warm shower, and then a trip somewhere for groceries. Let my new life begin," she avowed.

CHAPTER 3

Lauren spent the next week unpacking and getting acquainted with the Village. As she could in her small neighborhood in New York, she found that she could walk to almost everything in the Village and had no immediate need to shop for a car, even though there was a Ferrari dealership on one side of the main street in the Village and a Maserati distributor just across from it— not that she would ever be able to afford such luxurious vehicles, but they were fun to look at. And, although the traffic in the Village was not as horrific as in New York City, the availability of parking was a challenge. Most of the spaces along the streets were designed for parallel parking, a feat she had never fully mastered. She discovered, however, that she was not alone in this shortcoming. She frequently laughed when she watched visitors struggle to back their cars into tight spaces in front of her condo.

The Village is a favorite vacation destination for people from all over the world. They come to shop at the unique boutiques and galleries that line the streets and to watch the harbor seals in their natural habitat. There was always a steady flow of pedestrians, cars, and motorcycles that passed in front of her window, especially on the weekends. Southern California also has some of the most beautiful sunsets in the world, and, in the evenings, the rails along the walkway overlooking the ocean are constantly lined with people toting cameras of all sorts and sizes. All of them come hoping to see the illusive *green flash* that supposedly streaks across the horizon at the moment that the sun slips over

18

the edge. So far, she had not caught a glimpse of the mysterious streak, but she had enjoyed several drinks named in its honor at the local restaurants.

The only drawback that she had found to the Village was that everything was built on a hill that flowed down toward the ocean. She already had learned that she would have to improve her stamina to make it up the steep incline that led from the cove to the business and commercial district above. She now understood why there were benches all along the streets. So far she had been unable to make the climb without stopping at least once to catch her breath. It was easy to separate the long-time residents who walked the hill on a regular basis from the tourists and new residents. The natives whizzed up the hill without even breathing heavily while visitors and new residents, like her, were barely able to make it from bench-to-bench.

Her condo was coming together nicely, and she was beginning to feel comfortable in the new surroundings. As she unpacked her belongings, she purposely tossed away anything that reminded her of Derrick. She started a box that she labeled *Goodwill*. She tossed every picture, every gift that he had given her, and anything else that reminded her of him into that box and later hauled it to her basement storage bin until she could locate a Goodwill deposit center.

She was actually surprised at how little he had given her in their three-years together. She knew she had given him much more and wondered if he too had started a Goodwill box.

Once everything was unpacked and arranged to her liking, the condo began to feel like home. She had been lucky to find such a place given her limited financial assets. Thanks to her former boss, she secured a multi-year lease on the property from its owner, who was a friend of his.

The owner had moved to Europe, but he didn't want to sell the condo in case he decided to return to the United States. She didn't blame him for not wanting to sell such a wonderful place. The complex was facing the ocean on one of the most prestigious streets in the Village. The purchase price for property along the ocean started at one million and skyrocketed upward from there.

Her condo was part of a three story, u-shaped building with thirty-six units of various sizes. The condos on the west side of the complex had an ocean view, while the others overlooked the common courtyard and swimming pool. The courtyard was furnished with outside lounges, patio tables, and several barbecue grills that surrounded the swimming pool. Huge ceramic pots scattered around the courtyard contained tropical plants like the intriguing bird-of-paradise and miniature palms that provided a tropical atmosphere that appealed to Lauren.

Her new home was certainly more luxurious than her tiny studio apartment above an art dealer in New York where she never opened a window because of the noxious fumes from the traffic below and where the only plant life she saw, was a rather puny looking geranium on her windowsill that she had tried desperately to keep alive. But here, regal looking palm trees and beautiful flowering plants surrounded her everywhere she looked. And, best of all, awe-inspiring marine life and strange looking sea birds passed daily right in front of her window. Each morning, the pastel colors of the sunrise that were mirrored on the ever-changing surface of the Pacific greeted her. And each night, the burning orange and red from the sinking sun and the sparkle of the moon and stars on the rolling waves bade her goodnight.

She had not formerly met anyone in her complex other than the manager, although she did try to introduce herself to her neighbor. On the day after she had arrived, she had knocked on her neighbor's door to deliver some cookies that she had baked. Even though she had heard someone moving around inside the condo, no one had come to the door, so she left the cookies on the doormat. After she had gone back inside her condo, she had heard her neighbor's door open and then quickly shut again. Later that day, when she had gone out, she had noticed that the cookies were gone.

She didn't feel isolated or alone, though. From a distance, she had established two new friends: the elderly woman with the dog, whom she called Mary, and the pilot on the trike, whom she had dubbed as Rex. She had no idea what their real names were, but she enjoyed waving to them every morning as if they were lifelong friends. From her tiny veranda, she greeted the two of them as they passed by her window. They always appeared at the same time each day, and she made sure that she was outside at their arrival times to welcome them. Although she knew nothing about either of her new acquaintances, they provided a sense of connection and filled some sort of strange need in her for consistency. She would be glad when Monday arrived, however, and she would begin to establish connections with others with actual names and real lives.

CHAPTER 4

Lauren stared at herself in the large mirror above the sink in the master bathroom. "I guess that's as good as it's going to get," she said as she turned from side to side and then leaned in close to make sure there were no mascara smudges under her long lashes covering her dark eyes. She reached for her jacket and slipped it over the new, white silk blouse that she had purchased from one of the boutiques in the Village. She knew that she would only get one shot at a first impression with her colleagues at the museum, and she wanted it be a positive one. The black suit was her favorite—professional but not overly severe or prudish.

She reached around her neck to pull her loosely wrapped ponytail over her right shoulder. She decided to wear her long, dark and curly hair swept to the right side and held in place with a strand of hair wrapped around it at the nape of her neck so that it could dangle casually over her shoulder. She wanted a polished but casual look. She had also quickly learned that the moist sea air caused her hair to wildly curl the minute she stepped outside even after she had spent hours straightening it and lacquering it with mousse.

She picked up the small pearl earrings and slipped them into her ears. "Okay," she said once again glancing at the mirror. "Where did I leave my watch?" she muttered and found it laying on the sink in front of her. "Calm down, you're a nervous wreck." As she fastened her watch around her left wrist, she flipped it over to look at the time. "Oh, my gosh, time for Mary. I hope I didn't miss her. I need the boost that her sweet smile gives me."

She rushed down the short hallway into the living room and slid open the glass door. Stepping outside onto the verandah, she sucked in a deep breath of the fresh morning air. It was early, and the sky was a collage of soft blue, pink, and lilac that reflected on the ocean and created a sensation that she had just stepped into a Monet landscape.

"Good morning, dear," called Mary as she came down the street. "You look lovely. Big day?" she asked.

"First day on a new job," called Lauren.

"Well, you look very nice. I used to be able to wear high heels like you're wearing, but not anymore. I'm sure you will 'wow them' as you young people would say." She then turned her attention to her dog that had sprawled out on the warm sidewalk and evidently had decided to take a snooze while they talked. "Come, Rochester," said Mary. "We haven't much farther to go." She turned once more toward Lauren and waved as she headed up the street.

"Rochester," repeated Lauren. "At least I have one actual name." Glancing down at her watch again, she knew she had just enough time to clear the table of her breakfast dishes before Rex would pedal around the corner. As she was about to go back inside, she heard a rustling sound from the slightly opened glass door of her neighbor's condo.

"I'd like to watch you walk up that hill in those stilettos," said a mocking voice from inside the door.

"Oh, my gosh, I forgot. Thanks for reminding me."

"I wasn't trying to be helpful," the voice responded.

"Whatever," retorted Lauren as she rushed to her bedroom to slip on her flats.

She quickly returned to the verandah just as Rex came around the corner.

"Look at you," called Rex. "All spiffed up and pretty! Going somewhere special?"

"No. New job and I'm nervous."

"Oh, you'll be just fine. I'm glad to see you're wearing sensible shoes, though. That climb up to the Village in those fancy, high heels that the young women wear today would be suicide for you and the shoes. I've seen lots of women staring helplessly at a broken off heel halfway up the hill. Well, good luck and knock 'em dead," called Rex as he pedaled away with his customary salute.

"If you're smart, you won't let them know you're scared," whispered the voice from next door.

"Shall I say thanks, or is that another sarcastic comment about my obvious nervousness."

"Take it however you like, but it's damn good advice," answered the voice.

Lauren was about to respond when she heard the glass door in her neighbor's condo slide shut. Now there's a story to be discovered, she thought. I wonder who she is. Oh well, she offered some good advice even if it was delivered with sarcasm.

She glanced once more at her watch and realized that she had just enough time to go over her welcome speech once more before she had to leave. Starting a new position is always a challenge, and she knew she would have to work her way into the culture of the Museum. She had carefully considered and practiced how she would introduce herself and describe her previous experience. She wanted to ensure her new colleagues that she was qualified for her new position without sounding egotistical or vain.

She already was aware that she would have to mend some hurt feelings with one of the assistant curators, Nathan Nordstrom, who had also been a candidate for her position. Although he had been at the Museum for more than five years, from the carefully phrased comments of Carl Cromwell, Director of the Museum, it was obvious that Nathan was not well liked among the powers that be.

"You'll have some fences to mend with Nathan," Dr. Cromwell had told her during her interview. "He can be a challenge, but he is also well liked by some of our more wealthy patrons, and the visitors love him. He's a stupendous tour guide and presenter, but his management skills are not up to the level that the job requires. Just make him feel important, and you'll get along just fine," he had advised.

"Time to leave," she said once more glancing at her watch. She heaved a long sigh, grabbed her briefcase, and stuffed her stilettos into its side pocket. She would wear her flats on her walk to the museum, but she needed her stilettos for confidence during the morning conference meeting. After another quick glance in the hall mirror, she headed out the door.

A woman was swimming laps in the pool as she passed by it, but she didn't take the time to say hello. She hurriedly crossed the courtyard and exited the door into the lobby. She glanced at the mailboxes but didn't check to see if she had any mail. Who would be writing me anyway—certainly not Derrick. Oh, not today. Don't think about him today. You have another arrogant male to worry about, namely Nathan Nordstrom, she reminded herself. Hmm. Nathan Nordstrom. I wonder if his parents planned the alliteration of his two names or whether he changed his name so it would flow musically off the tongue. My bet is that he changed it—another mystery to discover.

She quickly skipped down the three steps from the condo entrance onto the sidewalk and hurried down the short walkway under the building's deep green canopy. Looking up at the intimidating incline, she muttered, "OK, hill, this time I'm coming to the top without stopping."

CHAPTER 5

Lauren purposely arrived early at the Museum. She slid her electronic key through the magnetic reader and grabbed the large brass handle to swing the door open as soon as she heard the click of the lock.

"Good morning," greeted a voice coming from behind the large Guest Relations desk in the lobby.

Lauren was startled by the sound of a voice echoing in the cavernous lobby of the Museum. "Oh," she screeched and clutched her chest.

"Sorry about that. I didn't mean to startle you. I'm David Mesa, one of the security guards here at the Museum.

"I just didn't think anyone would be here yet."

"I'm always here early. I like to have some peace and quiet before the rush starts. It's the only silence I have during the day. I have five kids under the age of six at home, so I come to work early just to enjoy a little solitude, but if you ever meet my wife, don't tell her. She thinks I have to be here this early."

"With five little ones, I bet she understands and probably would like to trade places with you."

"I don't know how she does it, but I watch the kids every night while she takes a long walk along the ocean. By the time she gets back, I have the kids in bed."

"You are a thoughtful husband. I'm sorry to trespass on your privacy. Let me introduce myself. I'm Lauren Allen, the new Head Curator."

27

"I figured you were," replied David. "I recognized you from your security badge picture, though you're much prettier in person. Besides, no one ever gets here early except new employees, but that only lasts for the first week or so. Anyway, welcome. If you ever need anything, let me know. I'm pretty well informed about everything that goes on around here. Can I show you to your office?"

"No, I think I can find it. It's on the second floor, as I recall."

"Yes. It has the best view in the building. Here, let me get the elevator for you." He reached for the large ring of keys dangling from a chain on his wide, black leather belt and slid the keys around on the ring until he located the elevator key. "We keep the elevator locked on the second floor at night as a security measure." He pushed a small, strange-looking key into the circular lock on the front of the elevator control pad, turned it, and then pushed the up button.

Lauren could hear the sound of the elevator as it began to drop to the first floor. As she waited, she glanced up at the beautiful seven-pointed, star-shaped clerestory skylight designed to bring natural light into the inner space of the grand exhibition area.

"Amazing place isn't it?" commented David. "I suppose you already know the history of this building. If you look around this immediate area, you'll find several buildings that were all designed by the same architect."

"Yes, I have read the history of the Museum and of the architecture of the area, but words can never describe the beauty of this lobby. I fell in love with the Museum the first time I saw it."

"That's what keeps people coming back here. Well, that

and the exhibits, although I have to admit that I don't always understand some of the art," said David as he reached to hold back the door so Lauren could enter the elevator. "Well, I'd better let you get on with your day. By the way, if you ever get here before I do, I'm afraid you'll have to use the stairs to get to your office. Only the security guards have an elevator key."

"Thanks. I'll remember that," said Lauren smiling. "I'll see you later I'm sure. Have a good day."

"I hope you do too. I don't think I'd like to be in your shoes, though. You've got some real challenges ahead of you," he said as he removed his hand from the door, and it slowly drifted closed.

Lauren was stunned by his last remark. I wonder what he meant by that. Is the situation with Nathan Nordstrom common knowledge to everyone who works here, or is there more to my new job than what I was told? I hope I haven't made another bad decision. "I seem to be good at that," she muttered as the elevator door quietly slid open, and she stepped out onto the second floor.

As she entered her office, she hesitated in the doorway and stared out at the panoramic view of the ocean through the immense double wall of floor to ceiling windows. "Wow! What a view. I didn't remember it being so beautiful. I'll have to discipline myself to concentrate on my work instead of staring out at the horizon."

Promptly at 8:55, which was the appropriate five minutes early arrival time for a meeting, Lauren walked into the conference room. Dr. Cromwell greeted her and motioned for her to sit next to him at the head of the long oblong table.

Her heart was racing and pounding in her chest so hard

that she was sure that he could see it through her suit jacket. The words of her mysterious neighbor echoed in her head, 'Don't let them know you are scared.'

"Good morning, Lauren. Help yourself to some coffee and Danish, if you'd like," he said. "We won't begin the meeting for another few minutes until everyone is here."

"Good morning, Dr. Cromwell. It's nice to see you again," she said as casually as she could muster. She would have loved to have a cup of coffee, but she had no intention of moving from the security of her assigned chair. She opened the binder containing the agenda and minutes from a previous meeting and scanned quickly to see if her name was listed as an agenda item. There she was—first item on a lengthy agenda with a time of two minutes assigned to her. Two minutes! She was sure she didn't have two minutes worth of comments to make. Noticing that her hands were trembling, she quickly put them in her lap and inhaled a long, nervous breath.

"First meetings are always the worst," whispered a young woman who plopped down in the chair next to her. "Hi, I'm Crystal Carter, one of your assistant curators. Welcome to our gorgeous Museum. I'd offer to shake your hand, but I'm betting they're cold and clammy."

Lauren laughed. "You're right. I am a tad nervous, but I was hoping it wasn't obvious."

"I don't blame you for being nervous. You're taking on a lot of major messes around here."

There it was again—another warning about her job. Can Nathan Nordstrom be that hard to deal with? And, what's with the alliteration of names around here— Nathan Nordstrom, Crystal Carter, Carl Cromwell? Maybe I'll change mine to Lauren Lovelace. She smiled at how such a name would definitely be unacceptable to the wealthy patrons of the Museum.

"OK, folks," said Dr. Cromwell. "We have a lot to cover today, so let's get started. You received the minutes of our last meeting by email, and there's a copy in your folder. Are there any corrections or additions to them?"

As Dr. Cromwell paused long enough to determine if anyone wanted to offer any changes to the minutes, Lauren did a fast visual sweep of the faces of those seated around the table. That's him. Nathan Nordstrom in person. I recognize him from his personnel profile. He's not bad to look at, but with his hair slicked back and dressed in that expensive pin-striped suit, highly starched, white shirt and silk tie, he looks more like a gangster than an assistant museum curator. Surely, the salary of a curator doesn't support that kind of dress.

His dark brown eyes met hers, and she could immediately detect his disdain for her. He raised his eyebrows and cocked his head to the side, and then he looked away and chuckled as if he considered her unworthy of his attention.

"I'd like to introduce Lauren Allen, our new Head Curator for the Museum," said Dr. Cromwell interrupting her thoughts. "Lauren, why don't you take just a couple of minutes to tell us about your future plans for the Museum."

What? Future plans? That wasn't what I had prepared to talk about. "Thank you, Dr. Cromwell. It's a pleasure to be part of such a distinguished group of art enthusiasts," she stammered. "Well, as you and I talked about when I was here last month, I am primarily interested in overseeing two changes at the Museum. First, I hope to decrease expenses by focusing on creating exhibitions based on the Museum's current collection and thus

31

reducing the extreme costs of the constant use of traveling and loaned exhibits. Secondly, I intend to extend our outreach to patrons, artists, and visitors through more interactive exhibits onsite and online."

From the opposite side of the table, she heard a slight snicker. She turned and saw Nathan lean toward the woman seated next to him whom she recognized as Betsy Hannah, the educational curator. "Like that's innovative," she heard him loudly whisper to Betsy.

Glaring directly at him, Lauren continued, "While some may not find these ideas particularly innovative, it is the way our industry is headed, and currently, at our Museum, we are failing in both practices. I feel certain that by cutting expenses and creating innovative, interactive exhibits, we will protect the Museum's endowment, increase our paid admissions, and attract new artists and patrons, which I am sure you are all aware is the key to the continued success of the Museum itself."

The rest of the meeting was a blur as she faded in and out of attending to what was being said. She continued to watch Nathan out of the corner of her eyes as he smirked and rolled his eyes at the reports from others on the staff. One item did, however, instantly capture her undivided interest. Dr. Cromwell reported that there was no immediate information about the stolen paintings from the Museum's standing collection.

Lauren immediately leaned forward in her chair and stared in disbelief at Dr. Cromwell. She instantly realized the significance of what he was saying. Now, I get David's and Crystal's warnings. The primary responsibility of a curator is care of a museum's collection. Many head curators have lost their job over a failure to ensure the security of the standing collection.

Dealing with Nathan Nordstrom is simply a small, personnel problem compared to the necessity of preventing the theft of major works of art.

Theft from any museum's collection could potentially result in its demise if it failed to meet ethical standards to protect its collection. When a theft occurs, the museum and the public not only lose access to the stolen art, but the museum is liable for not ensuring the security of the collection. If one of the pieces of lost art was an accepted or loaned work, the lenders and donors could sue the museum. And, of course, the reputation of the museum is at stake. The international community of museums takes seriously a failure to protect any art under the stewardship of a public or private museum. Oh, my god, the problems in my life just keep piling up.

After the meeting, she watched Nathan and Betsy scurry to get out of the room before she could approach them.

"There they go," whispered Crystal, tossing her head toward the two of them. "Good luck catching them."

Lauren quickly grabbed her binder and raced into the hall with Crystal following close behind her. "Nathan, Betsy," she called. "Wait a second. I'd like to speak to you for a minute."

The two escapees slowed, and Nathan turned around but continued to walk backward down the hall. "Can't right now. I have a tour coming up in a few minutes."

"Me, too," said Betsy, who had stopped and turned to face her. Lauren noticed that Nathan immediately reached over and tugged on Betsy's jacket to signal for her to keep walking.

Lauren sped up to catch up with them. "Well, when are you free?"

"I'm booked all day," replied Nathan. "Maybe later in the week."

"I'm sorry, but I need to see you today. How about 5:00 in my office?"

"In case you don't know, we leave at 5:00," he answered with a laugh.

"Not today. See you both at 5:00 for just a half-hour or so. You, too, Crystal," she responded as she stepped onto the elevator.

"I'll be there," replied Crystal jumping into the elevator with her. "Do you have a few minutes to talk," she asked as the doors closed.

"Sure. I'd love to ask you some questions about the missing pieces of art from the Museum collection."

"I'm sure you would. That's one of the reasons Martha left. She was the previous Head Curator. I think the Board actually fired her for not reporting the thefts right away and for not being able to account for their disappearance. Didn't they tell you about this when they hired you?"

"No. This morning was the first time I had heard anything about it."

"Wow! That doesn't seem fair."

"No, it doesn't." She unlocked the door to her office and motioned for Crystal to go in ahead of her.

"I just love this view," said Crystal.

"Me too."

Lauren laid the binder on her desk and then turned to look at Crystal, who was leaning toward the glass window and trying to see farther up the cove. Lauren was impressed with the natural beauty of her young colleague. She was tall and slender with thick blonde, wavy hair that flowed to a point down her back just above her tiny waistline. She was wearing a floral sundress and a short, white jacket with a small, stand-up collar. The jacket was cut in a curve in front with short sleeves that barely covered her shapely and slender upper arms. She wore expensive looking shoes that matched the dark green leaves of the flowers in her dress. The small, wedged heel and open toe shoes exposed her beautiful French pedicure.

How do these people afford to dress like they do? I know their salaries, and there is no way they could afford to spend that much on their wardrobes.

From studying her personnel record, Lauren knew that Crystal had been recently hired at the Museum as an Assistant Curator responsible for procuring and maintaining connections with California artists and patrons. She had completed her Master of Arts degree in Art History from Berkley University several years ago and was just twenty-five years old. There was a gap of two years between the time she graduated and was hired last month by the Museum. No previous employment was listed on her employment record. I wonder how she managed to land this job without previous experience.

"So, Crystal, what is it that you wanted to see me about?" asked Lauren.

Crystal turned away from the window and stared for a moment at Lauren. She then walked over to the door and closed it. "You'll definitely want to keep that door closed," she said.

"Really? Why?"

"Voices from this office carry out into the hallway when

35

the door is open. The acoustics in the building broadcast your voice into Nathan's office down the hall. Martha found that out the hard way," said Crystal.

She then walked over and plopped down in a contemporary designer chair across from Lauren. Leaning forward and resting her elbows on the desk, she hesitantly muttered, "I'm not sure if I am about to do the right thing here or not, but I like you, and I would like to help you be successful."

"Thanks. I appreciate that. I could use a friend here; that's obvious."

"I don't want to appear like I'm trying to be a whistle blower or anything like that, nor do I expect any favors from you or anything. I just want to tell you what I've learned about the politics of this place in the short time I've been here, and I would like to help this become a more pleasurable work environment. Honestly, I don't think that will happen until Nathan Nordstrom is gone."

She hesitated for a moment to watch Lauren's reaction before continuing. "Of course, that will be rather hard to achieve since his aunt is one of the Museum's wealthiest patrons. I think that's the only reason he's able to keep his job, even though I have to admit that the guests love him as a tour guide. He's not the same person in front of a crowd. He's certainly a Jekyll and Hyde personality."

"I intend to catch one of his tours this afternoon," said Lauren. "I'd like to see the positive side of his character. So far he has managed to mask it."

Crystal laughed. "The only time you'll see his positive side is during a tour. You certainly won't see that faked, positive persona in the administrative wing of the Museum."

"Is there something more I should know about Nathan?

What is his relationship with Betsy? She seems to follow his lead."

"He has her thinking that he is her protector. He bullies her something fierce. I feel sorry for her. I think that she truly believes he cares for her. I guess they are dating, but believe me he's not a one-gal guy. I've seen him in the bars around town and in San Diego. He is a first-class, womanizing jerk."

"Do you think we can wean her away from him, so she'll be more likely to cooperate with us? Her role as the educational curator is certainly a critical one for the success of any exhibition we offer."

"I have a scheme that might work to accomplish two things at once—get rid of Nathan and win Betsy over to our side, but I haven't really got it all worked out in my mind yet, and I'm not sure you'll like it. But that's another conversation. What I wanted to talk to you about now is the new exhibition coming up."

"What about it?" asked Lauren. "It was my understanding that the details were all worked out for the switch coming up at the end of the month."

The phone rang and both women jumped. Lauren reached for the phone as Crystal got up and started to leave to give her privacy for the call. Lauren motioned for her to stay seated.

"Hello, Lauren Allen speaking," answered Lauren. "Yes, Dr. Cromwell. I'd be happy to join you for lunch. OK, then. See you at 12:30 in the Café."

"I'd better let you get to work," said Crystal as Lauren hung up the phone.

"No, wait. What were you going to tell me about the new exhibition?"

"That's probably what Dr. Cromwell wants to talk to you about—well, possibly that and about the missing pieces of art. Maybe, I should just let him tell you."

"Tell me what? Crystal, what is it?"

Crystal stared at her for a moment and then drew in a deep breath. "Well, I think you should know that the digital copy of the design layout for the new exhibition mysteriously disappeared from the network servers."

"What?" shouted Lauren as she sunk back into her chair. "How is that possible? Weren't the files password protected? Can't the techies recover them? Can't they track who erased them?"

"Let's see, which of those questions shall I answer first?" said Crystal. "I guess it doesn't matter because the answer to each one is no, no, and no. The system was hacked from the outside, and all of the current and former design layouts were wiped off the servers. And to make matters worse, the only hard copies of the layout for the new exhibition were stolen from that filing cabinet over there," she said pointing to the cherry, lateral file credenza next to the window behind Lauren's desk.

"Well, that certainly had to be an inside job. Weren't there any fingerprints? Are you sure that Martha didn't take them?"

"No, Martha was interrogated by Dr. Cromwell and by the police. I've also called and talked to her. She is too conscientious and honest to ever do such a thing. She told me she would be glad to tell you what she remembers about the layout, but as you obviously know, there's no way to keep all those intricate details in your head."

"You must have some idea of who would steal

something like that. Surely, Nathan Nordstrom is not that evil and clandestine, is he?"

"Yes. I think he is precisely the perpetrator. He doesn't care about the Museum, and he hates being a curator. I've heard him say so. I think he wants you and everyone else around here to fail miserably. Then, I would bet my life that he would ride in at the last minute to save the day, by applying what he claims to be his miraculous memory for details. Of course, he will let the rest of us drown first."

"The exhibit is to open in just six weeks. We close the Museum at the end of the month. Have the preparators been lined up? My good god, has anything been done? What about the marketing…what about the other smaller exhibits…oh, good grief," moaned Lauren leaning over and gently, pounding her head on her desk.

"Well, at least I've told you. You have just one hour to come up with a strategic plan before you meet with Dr. Cromwell. I'll go and grab what I have on the regional exhibits, and we can piece something together so you can avoid having your face fall into your salad when he tells you what he expects from you at lunch." She jumped up and headed out the door, carefully closing it behind her.

Lauren stared at the door still stunned from what she had just been told. She whirled around in her chair toward the ocean view. "Oh, my god," she said. "If I can't straighten this mess out, I may lose my job, then I will end up not only alone but also completely miserable."

CHAPTER 6

During lunch, Lauren listened quietly as Dr. Cromwell explained about the lost layout files. She knew she owed Crystal for her ability to reply calmly to his obviously rehearsed apology for not telling her at the time she was hired about the exhibition difficulties and the theft of the pieces of art.

"I really wanted you to accept our offer, and I was afraid if I exposed all of our dirty laundry at once, it would scare you off," said Dr. Cromwell.

"On the contrary, Dr. Cromwell, I like a challenge, and I am confident that, with Crystal Carter's help, she and I will be able to solve the design layout issue. I wish I could say the same about the cooperation of Nathan and Betsy, but their earlier response for my suggestion of a brief meeting today indicated their current hesitancy to come on board."

"I'm sure they will help out with this. They are aware of the expediency of a resolution to the design layout catastrophe, and Nathan has indicated that he can recall most of the details about the changes to the galleries."

"And, if they don't cooperate?" Lauren asked. She took a drink of her iced tea and watched Dr. Cromwell closely to observe his response to her question.

He looked directly at her, and she immediately detected impatience in his eyes. "Well, my understanding from your former boss was that you had excellent people skills and handled the divas of the art world effectively."

"Histrionic divas, I can handle," replied Lauren.

"Narcissistic obstructionists and love-blind dependents I haven't had a lot of experience with."

Dr. Cromwell burst out in boisterous laughter, causing several of the other Museum employees in the Café to turn and look at the two of them. When he finally regained his composure, he said, "Well, one thing about you is certain, you can quickly and appropriately categorize personalities." He chuckled again as he returned to eating his salad.

Lauren realized that he didn't answer her question. He obviously wasn't going to offer her any support in dealing with Nathan and Betsy, and so, she changed the subject. "The fortunate thing about the lost layout is that the new exhibition is a traveling one. I will immediately contact the other museums that have housed it and try to get as much help from them as possible. Most curators are willing to cooperate, and I happen to know several of the curators at Watkins. They showed the same exhibit in January."

"Excellent idea," said Dr. Cromwell. "Now about the theft of some of the pieces of art."

"I have already gone over the complete inventory of the current collection and have contacted the Chief of Museum Security. We are meeting tomorrow to review current security procedures outlined in the Resource Management Plan and to implement procedures to ensure that there is no opportunity for future theft. At the present, there appear to be no leads on the lost objects. I, of course, will assist with that investigation as much as I can, but I trust you will not hold me responsible for their loss."

Dr. Cromwell suddenly got very serious. He reached across the table and put his hand over hers. "Thanks, Lauren. I wasn't sure how you were going to take all of this. I was afraid that you might run out of the cafeteria screaming. You've made my day a whole lot brighter. I have a meeting with the Chairman of the Board in an hour, and I need to be able to assure him that we are on top of both of these issues. Thanks to you, I can now do that."

I guess my career is not the only one at stake in this debacle, she thought. And, if it hadn't been for Crystal, I might have run out of the cafeteria screaming. Maybe I should have given Crystal credit for my faked confidence, but I was afraid to disclose that she had already warned me in case it would reflect badly on her. Note to self: do something nice for Crystal.

After lunch, Lauren headed into the Museum galleries in search of Nathan. She knew he had a 1:00 tour, and she was hoping to find something positive about him that she might be able to say as an offering of peace at their meeting tonight. She finally caught up with him in the Ocean Gallery.

"Well, well, folks," announced Nathan. "We have been fortunate enough to be joined by the Museum's new Head Curator, Lauren Allen. Perhaps, Ms. Allen, you would be so kind as to tell us what you know about this artist?"

Lauren knew that he was purposely trying to embarrass her because the artist he was referring to was a new, Californian artist whose works had only recently been reviewed by the Board. He obviously assumed that she would know nothing about the artist or the painting, but he was wrong.

What Nathan didn't know was that the young artist was one of her former colleagues in graduate school and that when she had visited the Museum for her interview, she had actually recommended to Dr. Cromwell that he have

42

someone contact the artist and consider adding him as one of their exhibited, regional artists.

When she accepted the job at the Museum, Dr. Cromwell had told her that the Board agreed to exhibit one of the artist's pieces based upon her recommendation. Before she moved to California, she had contacted the grateful artist who sent her his digital portfolio. And so, as it turned out, she had actually selected the painting that the tour group was currently admiring.

"I would be glad to join you, Mr. Nordstrom," she said.

For the next five minutes, she led the visitors in an engaging dialogue about the painting and about the artist. She watched Nathan fume when the tour group actually clapped for her after she finished the presentation.

"Thanks, Nathan," she said with a smirk that she hoped portrayed the "gotcha" message that she wanted it to. "I appreciate you including me."

She continued to follow the group through one more gallery and had to admit that Nathan was knowledgeable and entertaining. He was able to inform his group about the various exhibits in a way that pointed out the significance of the piece of art, the peculiar style and media of choice of each artist, and the interrelationship between the different pieces of art and the overall theme of the exhibit. Yet, he did it without sounding esoteric and with just the right amount of levity to make the tour enjoyable for both the informed and uninformed about contemporary art.

Satisfied that she had seen enough to be able to sincerely praise his presentation, she headed back to her office. As she sat down at her desk, she noticed the blinking light on her desk phone indicating that she had a voice message. She picked up the phone and listened as Crystal's excited voice blurted out, 'Call me as soon as you get back.'

"Now what?" she muttered as she dialed Crystal's extension. "Hi, what's up?" she said.

"I'll be right over, if that's all right," responded Crystal.

"Sure, it is. Come on over."

Within seconds, Crystal bounced in through the open door. "I am serious about you needing to keep your door closed," she scolded as she closed the door behind her.

"I forgot. I'm not used to keeping my door closed. What's up? Please don't tell me there's more bad news."

"No, actually I have a gift for you," she answered as she slid a binder across the wide, highly polished desk.

Lauren picked up the binder and quickly scanned through the pages. "Where did you get this?"

"Don't get too excited. It's not our lost layout. It's the final design for the Watkins' exhibition. When you went to lunch, I took your suggestion and called Watkins and spoke to one of the curators there. Turns out that he is a friend of yours, so he was more than willing to fax us their layout."

"It must have been Tom Seymor. He's a great guy. You should get to know him."

"Well, he certainly sang your praises," replied Crystal.

Lauren smiled. "This is fantastic, Crystal. It'll save us gobs of time."

"I know. Look at the last two or three pages. I went ahead and sketched out a schematic for a couple of our

44

galleries without the temporary walls that we had added for the current exhibition."

Lauren carefully examined the drawn-to-scale layout of the panels for the Museum's two largest galleries. "This is amazing work. It's beautiful. You obviously have plenty of artistic talent of your own."

"Thanks. By the way, how was lunch?"

"Thanks to you, I was able to respond without falling face down in my salad. I think I left him with a sense that we could get everything accomplished and stay on schedule for the new opening. But, I wish I felt as confident as I let on to him."

"You didn't tell him that I had already told you about the lost design, did you?"

Lauren closed up the binder and looked over at Crystal. "No, I didn't, but I felt guilty not telling him how much help you have been. I know I owe you big time."

"No, you don't. I'm glad you didn't tell him. I wouldn't want him to think I was stirring up trouble."

Lauren smiled, relieved that Crystal hadn't expected her to tell Dr. Cromwell that she already knew about the lost layouts. "I did tell him that I knew I could count on you for support but that I wasn't sure about the other two."

"You did? What did he say?" Crystal leaned over the desk, obvious excitement glistening in her pale, blue eyes.

"He skirted the issue, but he made it clear that it was my job to get them to cooperate."

"Hmm. I was afraid of that. I think he's intimidated by Nathan's connections with the more powerful patrons of the Museum, too." She leaned back in her chair, apparently deflated and disappointed in Dr. Cromwell. "Well, I'd better get back to work. I'll see you at five," she said and slowly pushed herself up from the chair.

"Don't give up," said Lauren as she watched Crystal walk dejectedly across the room. "We'll make this work."

Crystal hesitated for a moment, and then she abruptly turned around and smiled. "Right, but I think it's time for Plan B."

"Plan B?" asked Lauren.

Crystal smiled mischievously. "More on that later. Don't forget, keep your door closed," she said as she quickly left Lauren's office. She closed the door again and then rattled the doorknob obviously trying to ensure that it was completely closed. Lauren chuckled and went back to studying the layout Crystal had given her.

The rest of the afternoon, Lauren walked through the galleries using Crystal's schematic design to determine the appropriateness of the lighting and space for the exhibits that she had sketched into each gallery. She was impressed with Crystal's insight about the flow of the exhibit and of the visitor traffic. She really is a Godsend, she thought.

By five, she was back in her office awaiting the arrival of the other curators. A light tap on her door raised her hopes that it would be Nathan or Betsy, but it was Crystal who poked her head in the door.

"Look out your window," she said pointing toward the window that overlooked the employee parking lot.

Lauren got up and walked over to the window. She could see a black Mercedes backing out of one of the parking spots. As the driver turned the car around in the narrow drive, Lauren recognized Nathan as the driver. Betsy was seated next to him in the passenger's seat. Nathan glanced up at her window. When he saw her staring down at him, he simply shrugged his shoulders and laughed.

"You have to be kidding me," she said whirling around to look at Crystal. "How can he be so flagrantly disrespectful?"

"That's Nathan," answered Crystal.

"That's just plain despicable." Lauren plopped down in her chair and folded her arms across her chest. "I really can't believe that someone could be so hateful."

"Do you still want to meet with just me?" asked Crystal.

"No. I guess not. You already know everything I was going to tell them. I'm going to take your layout home with me and try to put together a schedule of assignments for each of us and a fabrication and installation plan for the preparators."

"By each of us, do you intend to include Nathan and Betsy?"

"Sure, why not? We need their help, don't we?"

"I don't want to cut our noses off to spite our face, but I think it would drive them nuts if we left them completely out of all the planning."

Lauren got up and walked over to the closet to get her purse and briefcase. "That would be suicidal. You and I can't do everything that has to be done without their help—especially without Betsy's. She has to oversee the educational pieces and the directional and identification signage."

"I think Betsy will cave after a couple of days. Let's just

try it, and if she doesn't fold within a day or two, I'll incorporate Plan B. Then, I know she'll come on board."

Lauren kicked off her stilettos and slipped on her flats. "Are you ever going to tell me the details of your Plan B?"

"Not until it's absolutely necessary. See you tomorrow," called Crystal. "Think about my idea of excluding them while you're making your action list."

Lauren smiled and shook her head, "You're a troublemaker."

"No, I'm a realist. They aren't going to help us anyway, so why give them a chance to be obstructionists? Lock your door when you leave, and put a piece of tape on the outside at the very bottom, so you can tell if anyone opened it before you do in the morning."

"What?"

"I learned a lot from my dad about how to keep myself safe." She smiled and closed the door.

CHAPTER 7

Lauren stopped by *Amici's* on the way home and picked up her favorite artichoke salad. She was in no mood to cook. As she walked down the incline toward her condo, she glanced up at the beautiful sun as it was slipping quietly into the ocean. If she hurried, she would be able to watch the final moments from her verandah. She was hoping to get a picture of the green flash with her new camera.

Photography was her area of expertise. She had held several showings of her work in different galleries in New York. The income from her photographs had supplemented her rather meager salary from her former job as a curator. She hoped she could continue to sell her work in some of the small galleries in the Village.

As she entered the condo courtyard and turned toward the small, shared walkway that led to her front door and to the front door of her neighbor, a man came bursting around the corner and crashed into her. She flew backward and landed on top of one of the lounge chairs next to the pool. Her briefcase skidded across the concrete patio, and she tossed the plastic bag containing her dinner into midair. Unfortunately, it came down with a splash in the middle of the swimming pool.

"Oh, I am so sorry. Are you okay?" asked the man.

Lauren immediately attempted to pull down her short skirt that had managed to slide up well above her upper thighs. She glanced up at the extremely handsome man who was towering over her and scowling down at her.

"I'm terribly sorry," he repeated as he glanced at his

49

watch. "It's just that I am in a bit of a hurry."

"Well, don't let me keep you. I'm fine, but I can't say the same for my dinner," she said as she watched the plastic bag containing her much anticipated salad slowly begin to fill with water and sink.

"Here, let me help you up," he said extending a well-manicured and deeply tanned hand to her.

"I don't need your help. Don't you have somewhere you have to be?"

"Yes. Of course, I do. I see that your dinner was from *Amici's*. What is it or was it? The least I can do is to have them deliver another for you."

"It was an artichoke salad, but they don't deliver."

"They'll do it for me."

"Oh, really. Fine, then go ahead and prevail on them for preferential treatment for you and have them deliver another one to me. Now, if you'll excuse me, I intend to fish my dinner out of the pool before the bag messes up the filter." She grabbed the long handle of the leaf skimmer and headed toward the other side of the pool.

"Well, if you're sure you're all right."

"Please, just go," she replied.

She watched as he picked up her briefcase, brushed it off, and laid it carefully on the lounge chair. He then hurried across the patio and out the door to the lobby.

She finally managed to catch her dinner in the skimmer's net and pulled it over to the side where she could reach it. She grabbed the plastic bag containing her chlorine soaked salad and headed for the trash chute.

As she started down the small, covered hallway to her

condo, she heard her neighbor's door slam.

"Did you enjoy that, whoever you are? Perhaps you should teach your guests to be more considerate of others who share the same entranceway," she yelled at the closed door. Oh for heaven's sake. What is the matter with me? "I'm sorry about that outburst," she said in a calmer voice. "It's just that I've had my fill of arrogant, inconsiderate males today."

There was no response from her neighbor—not that she really expected one.

Finally, inside her condo, she dropped her briefcase in the entranceway and hurriedly ran to the sliding glass door to see if she had missed the last few minutes of the sunset. Unfortunately, she had, but the sky was still a panorama of brilliant orange. She drew in a deep breath and stood quietly trying to calm herself after a rather hectic and disappointing day. The soft sound of the waves lashing against the rocks below and the call of the seabirds as they headed back to their nightly roost were comforting. She continued to watch as the fiery orange faded and the softness of twilight crept across the ocean.

A sudden pounding on her door, caused her to jump. Who could be pounding on my door? No one knows where I live. The pounding continued and she yelled, "Coming, for Pete's sake, don't knock the door down."

She peeked out of the small door scope, and recognized the man who had just knocked her down. He was staring at his watch and anxiously swinging a white plastic bag back and forth. She quickly opened the door and had to duck to avoid being struck in the face by a massive fist that was about to pound on the door again.

"Yikes. That was a near miss. Are you intent on causing me bodily harm?" she asked. Then noticing the *Amici's* bag, she added, "So, *Amici's* won't deliver, even for you."

"Right. So here," he said, thrusting the bag at her

"You really didn't have to do this," she said. "I can cook when I am in the mood or when it is necessary."

"Just take it. Now, I am really late for an appointment."

"Then, adios again," she said. "Oops, I guess I should add a thank you."

"Not necessary," he said and whirled around rushing into the courtyard.

"Slow down. You might have to deliver another dinner to someone else you annihilate," she called.

She was about to close her door, when her neighbor called out through a small, open crack in her door. "Don't go getting ideas about him. He's not interested in getting ripped off by another, money-grabbing woman."

"Don't worry," responded Lauren. "I'm through with romance." Hesitating for a moment, she turned toward her neighbor's door. "Are we ever going to meet like normal neighbor's do?"

"Hope not," answered her neighbor slamming her door.

CHAPTER 8

For the next two weeks, Crystal and Lauren worked together to complete the schematic diagrams for each gallery and each exhibit. Lauren met with the Chief Preparator who oversees all the demolition and construction when one exhibition closes and another opens. She was relieved that, with just a few modifications, he was able to use the lighting and mechanical schematic that Watkins had provided.

She had decided to take Crystal's advice and did not include Nathan or Betsy in any specific way with the work on the exhibit, although she did email them a list of the meeting times that she had planned for work on the exhibition. She had blind-copied Dr. Cromwell on the email so that he would know that she had informed them about the schedule of meetings. As she had anticipated, neither Nathan nor Betsy showed up for any of the scheduled conferences. But, even without their help, Lauren was satisfied that they were going to meet the deadline of the scheduled opening; however, she continued to worry about the educational pieces and the signage for the various exhibits. Typically, that would be Betsy's responsibility.

She was on her way back to her office from a meeting with Dr. Cromwell where they had discussed the new security plans for the Museum's collection and had reviewed the final exhibition design before she was to present it to the Board next week. As she passed by Nathan's office, she could hear Betsy's voice. She sounded angry and upset.

Lauren hesitated outside the open door of Nathan's

office. Even though she was aware that it was wrong to listen to someone's conversation without him knowing it, she couldn't stop herself from eavesdropping.

"Quit being so paranoid," she heard Nathan say. "No one is going to get fired. I told you I have everything under control."

"But we're going to look like idiots in front of the Board next week when Lauren and Crystal make their presentation, and we have to admit that we were not part of any of their planning," Betsy argued.

You certainly will, thought Lauren. She started to leave but stopped short when she heard Nathan's loud, mocking laugh.

"Look, I've seen their plans. They're using something they evidently got from another museum, and it will never work here. They've also left out some of the key exhibits from our standing collection that we decided to incorporate into the traveling one."

"What exhibits are you talking about? I don't recall that we agreed to add anything from the Museum's collection," said Betsy.

"Of course, you don't remember doing that because we didn't add anything. But the Board doesn't know that, and Lauren doesn't know that."

"What about Crystal?" asked Betsy. "She'll know."

"She wasn't hired until the week before Martha left, if you remember. I'll just explain that the decision was made to add the other exhibits before she was hired. I've already selected a couple of our Warhol exhibits from the collection and built them into their design by simply modifying what they've already done. So, when I point out to the Board that they've left out some important exhibits, it will throw off their whole schematic. I will then show them our plan with the other exhibits appropriately incorporated.   Your task is to tell the Board why the additional exhibits are key to the success of the show. Then we'll look like heroes, and they'll look like fools."

It took all of Lauren's will power to keep from storming into Nathan's office and confronting the two of them. How in the heck did he get a copy of our layout? She immediately headed for Crystal's office.

She knocked once on Crystal's door, and then opened it before Crystal had a chance to respond. "You will never believe what I just heard," she blurted out.

"Close my door, please," said Crystal.

"Oh, of course," said Lauren going back to close the door. As she turned to face Crystal, she immediately began spewing out Nathan's conversation with Betsy. "How could they have gotten a copy of our layout?" she asked as she plopped down in the nearest chair.

"Did you put the tape on the bottom of your door like I told you to?" asked Crystal.

"No. I didn't."

"Did you lock your door each time you went out?"

"No. Look, I have key anxiety. I'm always afraid I'll forget my keys and lock myself out." Lauren knew it was a lame excuse, but it was true.

"Well, it's pretty simple then to figure out how they got a copy of our layout. Nathan just went into your office and copied it."

"You've got to be kidding me," said Lauren. She jumped up from the chair and began pacing back and forth in front of Crystal's desk. "I feel like I'm living inside of some cheap detective story."

"OK. We can no longer avoid Plan B," said Crystal. "So, here it is. Nathan is constantly hitting on me whenever Betsy is not around. He has asked me out dozens of times in the short time I've been here."

"So?" interjected Lauren. "I assume you're going to try to make Betsy jealous by telling her about his unfaithfulness. Surely, you realize that he'll just deny it and that she'll believe him, not you."

"I'm way ahead of you on that one, Lauren. I'm not naïve. I know she wouldn't believe me if I just told her, but…" she paused, and for dramatic effect, she walked around to sit on the edge of her desk directly in front of Lauren. "she will believe a video."

"What? And just how do you intend to get a video without him knowing it?"

"Don't worry about that. I have that all worked out." She picked up her iPad and waved it in the air. "You do know that you can reverse the camera on this marvelous piece of technology, right?

"Yes, but I'm sure Nathan knows that, too."

"But, if he doesn't know that I have the camera on, he won't know that I am recording him. Remember, there is no telltale red light that flashes on the iPad to indicate that you're recording, if you lightly close the case."

Lauren sat quietly for a moment. "OK, that might work to get Betsy to cross over to our side, but you had mentioned earlier that Plan B would kill two birds with one stone. How do you think your little scheme will get Nathan fired or make him quit?"

Crystal laughed with excitement and amazement at

Lauren's innocence. "Lauren, my dear," she said, "sexual harassment is taken very seriously these days, particularly in an environment like ours."

"Sexual harassment? I don't know," said Lauren. "You could be the one ending up in trouble. There are privacy laws and rules against entrapment too, you know."

"You don't have to worry about me. Nathan is not the only one who has a protector, although so far I have managed to avoid ever calling in my cavalry."

"Your cavalry?"

"Never mind about that; it's a long story that I prefer to keep private."

Lauren frowned. "Well, good for you, but I don't have anyone who will come to my defense. And, if this backfires, my neck is on the chopping block, too." She plopped back down in the chair and folded her arms across her chest.

"It won't fail. I promise," replied Crystal. "Anyway, are you okay with this or not?"

"I am against it," said Lauren. "I think it's too risky and could easily backfire on both of us."

"Good," said Crystal waving a small digital recorder in the air.

"My good grief," said Lauren exhaling a long sigh. "Did you just record this conversation?"

"I did record it—something else I learned from my father. Anyway, I recorded it for your sake, not mine. So, now you too have a fairy godmother."

"Unfortunately, however, my fairy godmother is simply a digital recording of temporary value for this situation only. Someday, I want to hear about your cavalry. Who is your father anyway, and what does he do for a living?"

"I don't usually share my personal background. It's safer that way, and I prefer to be judged because of what I personally accomplish, not because of who I am."

"My life has been immersed in one mystery after another since I moved out here. Nothing seems to be what it appears to be, including you." Lauren shook her head and slowly pushed herself out of the chair. She headed for the door and stepped out into the hallway. "See you later," she called.

"Close my door, please," reminded Crystal. "See you on Monday. Come ready for you know what to hit the fan, as Plan B is finally executed."

"I can't wait," muttered Lauren closing the door behind her.

CHAPTER 9

It was Saturday, and Lauren was looking forward to a weekend of rest away from the drama going on at the Museum. After tossing and turning all night, she had finally decided to call off the so-called Plan B. Even though she knew that it would probably bring Betsy into the fold, she wasn't sure that it would get rid of Nathan. In fact, she felt confident that it would most certainly backfire and that Nathan would manage to use the whole affair to get rid of her and Crystal.

Still in her pajamas, she stepped out onto her verandah to greet Mary and to enjoy the gorgeous morning sky. As she drew in a deep breath of the fresh morning air, she glanced over at her neighbor's sliding glass door. The slanted blinds were drawn shut. Good. *Maybe I can avoid her sarcastic remarks this morning.*

She gazed out at the long line of cormorants that fly each morning from the far end of the cove where they roost, out toward the ocean for their early morning feeding. Each day, the long, straight line of the large, pelican-like sea birds fly low over the ocean in front of her condo in a continuous parade that lasts for more than ten minutes. She tried to count the birds once, but gave up after she had counted over two hundred of them, and the end of the line was still not in view.

Suddenly aware of the time, she glanced down at her watch. "That's weird," she said aloud. "Mary's late. That never happens." She leaned out over the wrought iron railing surrounding her verandah to see if Mary was walking toward her condo.

"Watch out. You might fall over that railing," called Rex as he pedaled around the corner.

"Good morning. I was looking for Mary," answered Lauren. "Have you seen her?"

"Who?" asked Rex.

Lauren smiled when she realized that Mary was not the woman's real name. "You know," she answered, "the older lady with the Boston terrier."

"Don't know her."

"You must have passed her on your way up the cove. She walks by here every morning."

"Sorry, can't say that I've ever noticed her, but I'll watch for her and tell her you're looking for her. What did you say her name was?"

Lauren laughed. "I really don't know what her name is, but her dog's name is Rochester?"

"OK, then," he answered. "By the way, my name is Dan. What's yours?"

"Lauren. Lauren Allen. I'm the Head Curator at the Museum."

"Really? Now, that's interesting," said Dan. "I pegged you for a young business executive, and figured your name would be more like Elizabeth or something like that."

Lauren laughed again. "I thought you looked like a Rex," she called out.

Dan burst out laughing. His entire body shook so hard that Lauren thought he might tumble off his trike.

"Close," he finally muttered. "That was my stage name,"

he said as he pedaled away.

Lauren could hear him still laughing even after he had disappeared out of her sight. Before going back inside, she looked down the street once more to see if she could spot Mary and Rochester. Seeing no one she recognized, she turned around to head back inside. As she passed through her kitchen, she heard a tremendous crash followed by a string of expletives coming from her neighbor's condo.

She immediately ran out into the entranceway and frantically knocked on her neighbor's front door. "Are you all right?" she called through the door.

"No. I'm not all right. I'm stuck, dammit," yelled her neighbor.

"Stuck? What do you mean you're stuck?"

"Oh, for Pete's sake. Everyone knows what stuck means."

Lauren chose to ignore her demeaning comment. "Are you in pain; are you bleeding?"

"No. I'm not bleeding, but I am uncomfortable, which is a normal condition of being stuck."

"How can I help you?"

"If you feel you have to help, call my son—903-002-3300, and don't ask me any more ridiculous questions."

"Are you sure you don't want me to call the condo manager, or 911?"

Another expletive sailed through the closed door followed by, "What part of 'call my son' didn't you understand?"

"But I thought the manager could get here quicker. I'm

sure he has a key."

"He plays golf every Saturday. Haven't you learned anything about this place?"

Lauren sighed and rushed back into her condo to grab her phone. Hastily she tapped in the number she had been given. Please, let this be the right number. I really don't want to have to ask her to repeat it again. She waited impatiently as the phone on the other end began to ring.

"Dr. Livingston," answered a male voice that sounded slightly out of breath and vaguely familiar to Lauren.

"Dr. Livingston, this is your mother's neighbor. At least, I hope I have the right number," she added.

"Are you the young woman I knocked down the other day?" asked Dr. Livingston.

"Thank, god," said Lauren. "I really didn't want to have to ask her again for your number."

Dr. Livingston laughed. "Is she Okay?" he asked.

"She's stuck," replied Lauren.

"What do you mean she's stuck?" asked Dr. Livingston.

Lauren smiled. "She didn't elaborate; she just said that she was stuck and told me to call you."

"Of course, she did. There's a key in a magnetic box at the bottom of the metal screen on her front door. Maybe you can use it to help her until I get there. I'm just around the corner. I was on my way over there to have breakfast with her anyway."

Lauren went back to the entranceway and tapped on her neighbor's door again. "Your son is on his way," she called. She leaned down and ran her hand along the bottom of the metal screen door. "He said there was a key in a magnetic box on your screen, but I can't seem to find it."

"Of course, you can't find it. I took it off the same day he put it on there. Just go away. I'm sure he'll be here soon."

Lauren sat down on the doormat with her legs crossed under her. "I don't want to leave until he gets here. I'll sit out here until he arrives just in case you need me to do something else."

"Go away. I don't need your help."

"I'm staying," said Lauren.

"Oh, for heaven's sake. You just want to get another chance to see my son."

Lauren couldn't believe what she was hearing. "I couldn't care less about your son. I just want to be close in case you need something."

"Like I believe that," answered her neighbor.

Lauren sighed. "Let's not talk. Just know that I'm out here in case you need me."

"Go away," shouted her neighbor again.

A rustling from behind her caused Lauren to swing around. She immediately recognized Dr. Livingston. From her position on the ground, he looked taller than she had remembered. His expensive looking jogging suit clung to his body like it was painted on him. His broad shoulders and thin torso made it appear that he was a perfectly sculptured statue rather than a mere, extremely handsome mortal.

He extended his hand to her to help her off the ground.

63

"It seems as though I'm always helping you up," he said with a broad smile.

Lauren felt a strange tingling sensation in the hand that he had held when he helped her up.

"Cody? Is that you?" called her neighbor.

"Yes, Mom. We're coming in to help you."

"Don't you dare let her in here. You know how I feel about that."

Cody turned toward Lauren. "Don't pay any attention to her. Her bark is much worse than her bite."

"That's all right," Lauren stammered. "I won't go in with you."

"No. Please do. I may need your help getting her unstuck, whatever that means."

"Well, if you say so. I don't mind helping out." She reached up and tried to smooth her hair that, from her shadow on the condo wall, she could tell was wildly sticking up in all directions.

Cody opened a leather bound key case with a Ferrari crest stamped across the front of it. He pulled out a large key and stuck it in the lock of his mother's door. "Mom," he called. "We're coming in. Where are you?"

"I'm in the exercise room, and don't you dare bring her in here."

Lauren looked up into Cody's smiling, gray eyes. "I'd better just go," she whispered.

"Nonsense. It's time you two finally met."

As they exited the narrow hallway that led to the main part of the condo, Lauren gasped at the size of the massive open space in front of her. It was at least quadruple the size of her living room. Off to one side of the main room was a narrow, spiral staircase that obviously led to a second floor.

She must have purchased the entire first and second floors of at least two units and converted them into one humongous one. No wonder I haven't seen anyone coming and going from the other condos along this side of the building. The units all belong to her.

She followed Cody through a huge, modernized kitchen and down the hall into an exercise room that was paneled with floor-to-ceiling mirrors on three walls and several sliding glass doors on the exterior wall overlooking the ocean.

"Good grief," yelled Cody. "What happened, Mom?"

Lauren stepped back out of the view of the petite, older woman lying on her back beside an electric bicycle.

"My stupid shoestring got wrapped around the pedal and pulled my shoe so tight that I can't get it loose. I tried to break the lace, but it was too strong."

"I'll get a knife from the kitchen," Lauren blurted out. She quickly covered her mouth with her hand and stepped backward so that her neighbor couldn't see her.

"What is she doing in here?" snarled her neighbor.

"Calm down, Mom. You'll cause your blood pressure to rise by being so hateful." He turned toward Lauren and said, "Good idea. Go get me a knife."

Lauren rushed into the large kitchen and dining area and quickly grabbed a kitchen knife. She hurried back into the exercise room and watched admiringly as Cody skillfully cut the shoestring that was dangerously close to his mother's foot.

"There you are, Mom. You're unstuck. Here, let me help you up."

"I can get up by myself. I'm not decrepit, just old." She hobbled past Lauren and headed into the living room where she plopped down on the largest white leather, sectional sofa that Lauren had ever seen. "Well, what are you waiting around for?" she shouted at Lauren. "The show's over."

"Mom, for heaven's sake," said Cody. "Behave yourself. You should thank her for helping you."

"What did she do for me? She just dialed your number. You were on your way over here for breakfast anyway. I could have waited, but she just kept pestering me to help, so I let her dial your number. That was probably a mistake. Now that she has your number, god only knows how much she'll pester you."

Lauren continued to stare at her neighbor. She immediately realized that there was something familiar about her pretty face and eyes. It was almost as if she had seen her somewhere before, but she knew that was impossible. "Well, I guess I'll be leaving," she finally said. "I'm glad you weren't hurt, but a little more time without circulation to that foot, and you might have been in worse trouble."

"I doubt it, but I'm glad you finally decided to leave. I'm sure you have something you need to do, like get dressed and comb your hair, maybe?"

Lauren turned to leave and caught a glimpse of herself in the hall mirror. Her hair was wildly curled and sticking up every which way, and she had forgotten that she was still in her pajamas. Horrified at her appearance, she turned around to look at Cody. "I apologize for the way I'm dressed, but I was just on my way to get a shower when I heard your mother's call for help."

"I did not call for help," corrected her neighbor. "If you heard anything, it was a string of my favorite expletives."

As Lauren turned to leave again, something caught her eye below the mantle of the huge fireplace in the living room. She stopped abruptly to stare at the golden statues inside of a glass enclosure.

"Now what?" asked her neighbor. "Haven't you ever seen an Oscar before?"

"Only on television," muttered Lauren awestruck by the display of Oscars staring back at her through the glass. "Oh, good grief. I know why you look so familiar. You are Lynette Starr."

"That is not my name. It was a pseudo name made up by my ridiculous agent."

"Her given name is Barbara Livingston," said Cody.

"I used to watch your movies with my mother when I was a child. I thought you were…"

"Dead?" interrupted her neighbor. "I'm not that old, for Pete's sake. And don't you dare tell anyone where I live. I chose this condo in this rather unimpressive neighborhood because no one would suspect me to be living in such a meager place. I don't want paparazzi stalking me and snapping pictures of my aging body. I want my privacy, do you understand that?"

"Oh, you don't need to worry about me telling anyone about you. I certainly wouldn't want the rest of your adoring public to realize what a bitch you really are," said Lauren as she rushed down the hall.

"Well, I never," shouted her neighbor.

Cody burst out laughing. "You deserved that, Mom," Lauren heard him say.

CHAPTER 10

Crystal searched through her considerable wardrobe trying to decide which of her many expensive dresses she would wear for her enactment of Plan B. She wanted to look seductive, but at the same time, she had to look professional for work—not an easy appearance to pull off. Finally, after rejecting half of her closet she found the dress she was looking for. "This one's perfect," she said grabbing a light blue sundress with off-the-shoulder cap sleeves and a fitted waistline.

I swore I would never wear this dress to the Museum again because the last time I wore it, Nathan cornered me in my office saying, 'that dress is perfect for your eyes and your shapely figure. It really turns me on.' "Yuck," she groaned. "He is without a doubt the most disgustingly sleazy person I have ever met. Plus, he's a bully, and I detest bullies."

As she was contemplating which of her dozens of pairs of shoes to wear, her private cellphone rang. She quickly grabbed it and answered it. "What's up, Dad?"

"Hello, sweetheart," answered her father. "I was just missing you and wondering how everything was going with your new boss."

"She's really great. I like her a lot. She's got real gumption."

"Like you," replied her father. "I pity the powers that be at the Museum. And what about our sleazebag target? Have you found out everything we need to know about his involvement in the theft?"

"I'm finally going to implement my Plan B that I was telling you about. Hopefully, by tonight he will be ours."

The voice on the other end of the line was silent for a moment.

"Are you still there, Dad?"

"Yes. I'm here, but I'm not so sure that you should carry out your plan so soon. You haven't any hard evidence about his sideline activities. If he suspects that you might be on to him, he's likely to become vicious. People like him always retaliate. Maybe I should send some reinforcements your way for a while."

"Dad, you promised you wouldn't interfere. I wanted to prove to you that I am capable of carrying out this assignment on my own. Besides, I know that you've already sent Jake and Tom out here, so they have my back."

There was nothing but silence again for several moments on the other end of the line. Finally, her father answered, "How did you know that Jake and Tom were out there? Did they contact you?"

"No, of course they didn't. But you trained me well. I can spot a tag a mile away."

"You know it's hard for me to stay out of your assignments, especially when I think you might be in danger. Why must you insist on being so damned independent?"

Crystal smiled. "You should know. I am your daughter after all, and there's no one who bucks the system more and who is more independent than you are."

Her father laughed. "I can't deny that."

Crystal glanced down at her watch. "Look, Dad, I do

70

have everything well planned out, but I want to get to the Museum early today to pull-off Plan B before Lauren has a chance to tell me to cancel it. She wasn't wholly on board on Friday, and she probably has mulled it over all weekend and may have decided to call it off. I realize that Nathan is not the ultimate target in all of this, but I know that he is so greedy and egotistical that my plan will force him to show his hand. He's just a piggish, quasi-intellectual creep who is so stupid that he doesn't know how much danger he really is in. But, trust me, I have it all under control. In fact, I'm enjoying this assignment so much that I may just plan to stay on forever. After all, I was trained as an art expert."

Her father exhaled a long, exasperated sigh. "Don't forget that your training in art history was for a broader purpose than working as a curator in a museum. However, I think your mom would be happier if you would use your talents that way. Say the word, and I will pull the plug on your role in the entire operation."

"Don't you dare. I especially want to see this one through to the finish. I want to be the reason that Nathan Nordstrom is going to rot in jail among the other art thieves who make the lives of legitimate artists and art enthusiasts miserable. He's a real low-life dressed in fancy clothes and pretending to be a fan of the arts."

"Don't get emotionally involved with wanting to trip him up so much that you let your guard down. Quasi-intellectuals like him were among the most treacherous criminals I ever tracked. So, don't turn your back on this guy."

"Point made, Dad," answered Crystal trying not to sound impatient.

"Sorry, I didn't intend this call to turn in to a lecture. I just hate it that you're so far away. Your mom and I miss

71

you terribly. It's been almost six months since we last saw you."

"I miss you, too. I promise to call you tonight and let you know how things went. Right now, I've got to get going. I want to get this over early before Lauren chickens out and calls it off."

"I hope she doesn't get too involved and end up in the middle of something that she can't handle."

"Don't worry, Dad, I've got her back."

"It's your back and getting the job done that I care about. You need to stay focused on our goal. Lauren is not your concern. Find those paintings and come home."

Crystal frowned. "That sounds insensitive," she said. "Anyway, I've got to go. Give mom a hug for me."

"Be careful," shouted her dad.

"Got it, Dad, good bye."

She tossed the phone on the bed and finished dressing quickly. She knew her parents worried about her, and they wished she had not chosen to follow in her father's footsteps as a private detective. But that was all she had ever wanted to do ever since she understood what her father did.

Although he had a Harvard law degree, he founded his own detective agency as soon as he passed the bar examination. His one-man operation quickly grew into a vast, profitable agency with locations on five continents and contracts from huge corporations, insurance conglomerates, governments from nations all over the world, and wealthy private individuals. The insurance company for the Museum had hired him when the missing art pieces were first discovered. One of the works that was stolen was the most valuable piece in the

Museum's entire collection.

Her specialty in her father's agency was art fraud and art theft, so she was the obvious choice for this investigation. She was a talented artist herself and committed to combining her love for art with her desire to prosecute those who would try to steal or destroy the beautiful works of famous or start-up artists. Working behind the scenes with the insurance company and the chairman of the Museum Board, she was hired as a curator; however, no one at the Museum, including Dr. Cromwell, was aware of Crystal's true identity.

Rushing out of her apartment, she walked the short, six blocks to the Museum. It was another beautiful morning in southern California, and she was feeling confident about her ability to successfully carry out Plan B.

As she walked past the black SUV parked on the street in front of the Museum, she struck the side of the van with her fist, and bent down pretending to fix her shoe. "Good morning, fellows," she whispered.

Tom Allen and Jake Cromley, the two males in the front seat, jumped and cursed. "How the heck did you know it was us?"

"I was trained by your boss," she answered with a quiet laugh. "Stay close, I'm going to start the ball rolling today."

"It's about time," muttered Jake. "All of this California sunshine is getting on my nerves. I prefer the snow and gray days of D.C."

"You do not. I know you better than that," she responded. She stood up and winked at the silhouetted face being the dark tinted passenger window. "Gotta go. The creep has landed."

Nathan was just pulling into the employee parking lot. Good, she thought. She quickly reversed her iPad's camera, set it to video, and pushed the record button. She then carefully closed the cover over the screen and headed toward the back entrance of the Museum where she knew Nathan would enter. Luckily, Betsy wasn't riding with him this morning, but that meant that she too would be pulling into the parking lot shortly. Crystal was certain that Nathan wouldn't reveal himself in front of Betsy or any of the other employees.

She picked up her step so that Nathan would see her coming down the driveway.

"Good morning," hailed Nathan. "What an unexpected pleasure seeing you this morning. And, you're wearing my favorite dress."

Crystal faked a smile but said nothing. She didn't want it to appear on the video that she did anything to encourage him.

"When are you going to give me the chance to see what's under that expensive dress?" he asked with a repulsive grin.

"Never," she responded. "And I don't appreciate those types of comments." She slid her magnetic key across the reader and reached for the door handle, but Nathan grabbed it first.

Giving a low, sweeping bow, he motioned for her to go in ahead of him. "I want to get the rear view of your voluptuous figure," he said.

Crystal immediately turned around to face him so that the camera was pointing directly at him. "Stop it, Nathan. I resent your sleazy remarks. And besides, aren't you dating Betsy?"

"We don't have an exclusive arrangement. Anyway, I've seen what's beneath her clothes, and I am certain that what you have under that beautiful dress is much..."

"You're disgusting," said Crystal interrupting him. And, I got you, she thought.

"You're not fooling me, Crystal. I've seen you looking me over. Sometimes it makes me feel a little uncomfortable—so much so, in fact, that I could report you for sexual harassment, you know."

Crystal seethed with disgust. "That's a lie, and you know it. You're insane. You're the last person in this world that I would ever give a second look."

"Well, it would just be your word against mine, and I've got considerable more clout than you do around here."

"How can you be so repulsive? No one would believe you. Everyone knows, except you, that I can't stand you," she said.

"Well, if you don't want to test my intentions, why don't you meet me tonight after work for drinks and whatever..." he said. He exposed the tip of his tongue, ran it across his lips, and ended with a demonic smirk.

"My good god," shouted Crystal, "you're even more revolting than I thought you were." She quickly turned away and ran up the back stairs to her office, slamming the door behind her. "Ooh," she said, shaking her body as if she were trying to rid herself of any residue of Nathan's vileness. Her phone buzzed, and she immediately grabbed it. "Hello," she shouted into the receiver.

"Crystal? Are you all right? You sound upset," said Lauren. "From my window, I saw you talking with Nathan in the parking lot."

"Sorry about that. I didn't mean to shout. I'm fine, but do you have time to see me right away?"

"Of course, that's actually why I called. I think we should talk again about this Plan B thing."

"I do too," answered Crystal. She grabbed her iPad and headed for Lauren's office.

When she entered, Lauren looked up from the pile of papers on her desk. "Wow, if that dress doesn't bring on a hit, then I don't know what would. You look sensational. But, unfortunately, I don't think we should go through with your plan. It's too likely to backfire."

Crystal smiled and slid the iPad across Lauren's desk. "Pull up the last video," she said.

Lauren's eyes got bigger and bigger as she listened to Nathan's disgusting remarks. "Oh, my god. I had no idea how revolting he is. There's no way he can deny this."

"It's a wonder I didn't hit him over the head with the iPad. Believe me, I was tempted."

"Now what?" asked Lauren. "What do we do with this?"

"First, I want to get the video copied. Do you have your iPhone handy? I'll airdrop it to you, and then I'll send it to you as an email attachment. We need to get it onto a DVD. I don't want to risk losing it before we need it."

"Good thinking," said Lauren. "Once he knows we have this, he will probably stop at nothing to get his hands on it and destroy it.

CHAPTER 11

Just as Lauren was about to leave for lunch, Betsy tentatively opened her office door and stuck her head inside. "May I have a minute with you?" she asked.

"Sure," said Lauren. "I was just about to go to lunch, would you like to join me?"

"No, thanks," answered Betsy. "I can come back later, if you'd prefer."

Lauren noticed that Betsy's eyes were red and swollen and suspected that Crystal had shared her video with her. They had decided that Crystal should be the one to talk with Betsy so that she wouldn't know that Lauren was also aware of the situation. "No, come on in. I can go to lunch later. Have a seat," she said pointing to a chair.

Betsy hesitantly entered the office, closing the door behind her. She sat down on the edge of the chair and stared down at her hands that were nervously twisting a tissue around her index finger. On her lap was a folder marked *New Exhibit.* "I'm not sure exactly where to start," she muttered.

Lauren didn't respond but got up and walked around her desk to sit in the chair next to Betsy. She reached over and laid her hand over Betsy's nervous ones. "Take your time," she said.

Betsy looked up and directly turned to face Lauren. "First," she mumbled, "I want to apologize for the way I have been treating you. I don't know what I was thinking."

Lauren smiled but didn't reply.

"I would really like to be part of whatever planning is left to do for the new exhibit. I have already laid out the catalog, the other advertisements and educational pieces, and the press kits. I also have designed most of the labels and other signage. I knew you would be worried about these pieces."

"You're right. I was concerned about them. But, how did you know how the layout would look? Without a copy of the layout, it would be impossible to anticipate the signage and labels." Lauren watched as Betsy squirmed in the chair.

"I'd rather not say how I knew about the layout. I'm sorry, but does it really matter how I learned about it?"

She's still going to protect that sleazebag, thought Lauren. She must really be in love with him.

Poor girl. I know the pain she is feeling. "I guess it doesn't matter. After all, I would have gladly shown you our layout if you'd have just asked."

"Again, I'm sorry about that, it's just that... Well, let's just leave it at, I'm sorry." She dropped her head and hesitated for a moment. Suddenly, her head snapped around and she looked up again at Lauren. "I really need this job," she said as if she were pleading for her life. "You probably don't know that I'm a single parent, and if I lose this job, I don't know what I'll do. I truly love my work here, and I know, when my head is on straight, I'm good at it. I promise I won't be resistant to your authority ever again. I actually hated not being a team player. It went against everything I am and believe."

Lauren was completely caught off guard by Betsy's disclosure. She didn't know that she had a child. There was nothing about that in her personnel record. She reached out and put her hand over Betsy's trembling ones. "I accept your apology, and I can assure you that I don't hold grudges. I've made some personal relationship mistakes in my life, too. And, you are right. I didn't know you had a child. Boy or girl? How old?"

"I try to separate my personal life from my professional life. Only just a few people from the Museum know about my baby. Her name is Maria." As she continued to talk about Maria, Betsy's eyes glistened with love and pride. "She's just three months old. No one even knew I was pregnant because I was so careful about my weight and about how I dressed. Dr. Cromwell knows and Susan from personnel, but no one else. Of course, now you know. But, please, I would appreciate it if you wouldn't tell any of the others. Please."

My good god, I wonder if Nathan knows. He's probably the father. What a mess we can make of our lives, all in the name of love. "I promise. I won't say anything to anyone else, but may I ask why you don't want the other's to know?"

Betsy's head again dropped to her chest and the twisting of the tissue around her finger quickened. Finally, she looked up and confidently stated, "I'd rather not explain my reasoning."

"Of course," said Lauren somewhat taken aback. "I shouldn't have asked, but along life's way, I have learned that it is sometimes better not to try to carry your burdens alone."

"I have the Lord as my confidant. And, I can trust that Source," replied Betsy with conviction.

"You certainly can," said Lauren patting Betsy's trembling hand. "I didn't mean to invade your privacy. But, if you don't stop twisting that tissue around your finger, you'll likely to create a paper mache` cast.

Believe me, I know it can happen. I did it during my orals for my doctorate."

Betsy laughed. "Seriously?" She quickly pulled her finger out of the tightly twisted tissue and got up from the chair. Before leaving, she turned once more toward Lauren. "Thanks, Lauren, for being so gracious. I promise; you won't be sorry. I really am a good educational curator and typically a team player."

"I'm sure you are. Thanks for your apology and sharing your personal life with me. I'm looking forward to a positive relationship with you, and I'm confident that we can get this exhibition open on time and show it off the way the art deserves."

"Oh, I almost forgot. There is something else I should share with you. I think that you might want to consider adding a couple of pieces from our Museum collection to the current layout. Here," she said handing Lauren the folder she had held in her hand. "I took the liberty of sketching a redesign of two of the galleries to accommodate the additions. You'll also find my rationale for why I think that they would enhance the original exhibit."

"Thanks, Betsy. I'll take a look at this, and if it won't cause the preparators too much additional work, then I'll add them."

"And, one more thing. You may think this is odd, but I have my reasons for asking," added Betsy.

Lauren stared at her. She was pretty sure she knew what Betsy was about to ask. "What is it?"

"Please don't tell Nathan that I talked to you. As you know, he's still pretty angry about being overlooked for your position, but I am confident that he'll eventually come around. Anyway, I'd rather tell him myself that I have talked with you."

Just as I thought, she is still going to try to shield him. "Sure. I won't mention our conversation to anyone but Crystal. I do have to let her know that she can stop worrying about the educational end of the exhibit."

"She knows. It was her idea that I come to see you. She's a good person and has a lot of confidence in your ability to handle challenges. Now, I know why she feels that way." She quickly turned and left the office, but immediately came back to close Lauren's office door. "You'll want to keep this closed," she said.

Lauren smiled. "Thanks for the reminder."

After Betsy had left, Lauren reached for her purse with the intention of heading for the Café. As she was about to leave, her phone rang. "Hmm." She turned around and stared at the monitor on her desk phone. "It's an outside call. I wonder who could be calling me." She hesitated a moment then picked up the phone. "Lauren Allen, speaking," she said.

"Well, Lauren Allen, I just happened to be in the area, and I was hoping that you hadn't already had lunch."

Lauren immediately recognized the deep, sexy male voice. "Dr. Livingston?"

"Yes, but I prefer that you call me, Cody. If you turn around, you'll see that I am in your employee parking lot."

Lauren quickly whirled around and glanced through the large window at the parking lot below. A red Ferrari convertible was parked in the center of the driveway, and she could see Cody Livingston smiling and waving his cell phone in the air.

"Well, do you have time for a quick lunch, or not?" he

asked.

"How did you know where I worked?"

"Mom told me."

"I'm surprised that she knew where I worked and even more surprised that she would tell you about it."

Cody laughed. "I told you her bark is worse than her bite. Are you coming down for lunch, or not?"

"Actually, I was just going to grab a quick bite to eat in the Museum Café and then take a cab to the city. I have to check on some art pieces in the Museum storage facility."

"Perfect," replied Cody. "I'll join you in the Café, and then take you into the city. It's the least I can do after what my mother put you through on Saturday."

Lauren surprisingly felt a pang of disappointment. So, he's just trying to repay a favor.

"Well?" asked Cody again.

"Sure. That sounds fine, but do you have time for all of that? As I recall, you're always racing to some appointment."

"I close the office on Mondays, and my surgery schedule ended about an hour ago."

"OK, then. I'll meet you downstairs in the Café. By the way, parking spot number 3 is mine. It should be empty, but you'd better put a note on your dashboard. Security would definitely know that car isn't mine, and they don't hesitate to have cars, even Ferraris, hauled away."

"Will do. See you in the Café."

Lauren continued to watch Cody skillfully whip the

Ferrari into her parking spot. She stepped back away from the window when she saw him look up and smile at her. Quickly glancing in the mirror on the back of her closet door, she freshened her lipstick. Thank god I took the time to pull my hair into a ponytail, she thought. "Hold it," she said staring at herself in the mirror. "What's wrong with you? This is simply nothing more than a payback. Anyway, no more romantic relationships, remember?" A strange tingle of excitement made her shudder. "I'm hopeless," she admitted.

.

CHAPTER 12

Cody Livingston had thought of nothing else but Lauren ever since he had first knocked her down the evening that he was rushing from his mother's condo. He had tried to push her out of his mind because he realized that, if he did try to see her, it would mean that he would be heading down a path that he had sworn he would never go down again. But, after their brief encounter again on Saturday, he had confessed to his mother that he had never had an immediate attraction to anyone like he felt for Lauren.

"You know, Cody. I can't say that I blame you. She sort of draws you in," had responded his mother.

"Well, that certainly is a surprise, especially coming from you. I thought you hated her."

"I don't hate her. I just don't want anyone to know who I am or who I was, I mean. But, I have to admit that, despite her wild curls, she is very pretty, and it appears that she is a good person with a caring heart. That's what I like about her. No matter how hard I've tried, I haven't been able to discourage her from reaching out to me."

Cody shook his head at his mother's admission that she purposely pushed away anyone who attempted to befriend her. She was obviously determined to hang on to her adopted facade of nastiness, regardless of how she felt about someone. But despite her quirks, he knew that his mother was a good judge of character. Lauren was not only eye candy with a sharp wit and caring personality; she had a vulnerability about her that made him want to protect her.

He had decided this morning that it was now or never. If he didn't reach out to Lauren right away, he was afraid that someone else would snatch her up and then he would regret it. "No more sitting on the sidelines," he had said as he stared at himself in the mirror in the doctor's lounge at the hospital. "This time it's going to be different," he muttered trying to convince himself.

He had been burned before by women, who appeared to be interested in him, but were actually more interested in living the posh life that he could provide them. One in particular had been very good at hiding her true self, and he had actually asked her to marry him. "Good, old April," he said with a long sigh. I should have listened to my mother back then. She told me that April was only after my money, he recalled.

As it turned out, April was not only dating him, but she was also having an affair with a married surgeon from the Scripps Hospital in San Diego. Unfortunately, for April, he and the other surgeon were in the same specialty and met at a conference held at Scripps. After the professional meetings, he and the other surgeon met for cocktails. And, as men sometimes will do after having fully rehashed the conference presentations, they began to talk about the women in their lives.

It wasn't long before it became apparent to both men that the other surgeon's mistress was Cody's intended. After that, he avoided any relationship with women other than professional ones. But, a single life was not what he wanted. In spite of how he had watched the divorce of his own parents turn his mother into the unpleasant, bitter person she had become, he still wanted to be a husband and a father.

His mother wasn't always sarcastic and hateful. When he was a young child, regardless of all the demands on her because of her movie career, she had been a loving

85

wife and mother. That all changed when her movie career suddenly ended, and his father sought his fortune from the starlets that replaced her as the leading lady. With each passing year, it was becoming harder for him to remember how she used to be because of how she had now come to view and treat the world. But, he still had hopes that she would find something that would inspire her to reach out to the world again. Lauren was the only person that he had ever heard his mother say anything positive about.

But, today is not about my mother, he thought as he climbed out of the Ferrari. It's about me pursuing what I want from someone I think can help me feel the way I want to feel and be what I want to be.

He looked once more up at the window and smiled at Lauren. He chuckled as she quickly backed away, obviously embarrassed that he had caught her staring at him.

CHAPTER 13

Lauren nervously entered the Museum Café and spotted Cody. He had selected an isolated table at the back of the outdoor dining area. When he saw her, he immediately stood up and held out a chair for her at the small, intimate table.

His tall, well-toned, and statuesque body and his tanned, handsome face surrounded by his thick dark, curly hair caused others in the café to stare admiringly at him. His designer, blue linen shirt, tan slacks, expensive, sockless leather loafers, and diamond studded watch broadcast wealth. She could feel the eyes of the other women in the Café gazing enviously at her as she approached the table.

"Hello there," she called. "This is quite an unexpected surprise."

"I'd hoped you'd describe it as a pleasant surprise."

Cody leaned in close to her as she slid into the chair, and he effortlessly pushed it closer to the table. She could feel his breath on the back of her neck, and she struggled to avoid displaying a delightful shiver.

She realized that she had a bad habit of attributing too much significance to words offered as polite conversation, but the inference that he considered the present circumstance as *pleasurable* caused a strange sensation in the pit of her stomach.

Trying to make light of his remark and to avoid reading too much into it, she responded, "Well, the pleasantness of it depends on what happens next. Given our track

87

record of previous encounters, I am a little leery of assigning the word *pleasant* to meetings with you."

Cody laughed. "I guess you have a point there. So, I will do my utmost to make this meeting pure pleasure."

Lauren immediately became tongue-tied. What do I say to him? He is, after all, a stranger. I really don't know anything about him. She was grateful when the waitress appeared to take their drink order.

"Am I making you nervous?" Cody asked with a teasing smile. "I can sense a bit of uneasiness about you, which I have never noticed during our previous meetings."

"You know, I think you do make me nervous. You are pretty much of a stranger. And, I can feel the eyes of everyone in this room on us."

"Would you prefer to go somewhere else?" he quickly asked with genuine concern reflected in his pale, gray eyes.

"No. I'll get over it. Why don't we start by talking about the one thing that we have in common—your mother?"

Cody let out a roaring laugh. "You're kidding, right?"

"No, not at all. She fascinates me. She obviously was a better actress than I ever suspected, given her current disposition and the sweet, innocent characters she portrayed in the movies."

Another bellowing laugh from Cody attracted more attention to them. Then, realizing she wasn't laughing, he said, "Oh, my god, you are serious. Come on. I'd much rather talk about you."

"There's not a lot to tell about me, but I suspect there's a lot to tell about your mom," answered Lauren. She smiled up at the waitress who delivered her ice tea and salad. "Please, Cody. I really would like to know more about her, so perhaps we can become normal neighbors."

Cody leaned across the table and lowered his voice as if he were about to tell a deep, dark secret. "Well, to begin with, there is nothing normal about my mother, so you are wasting your time if you try to establish any sort of relationship with her. She actually hates most people, even me sometimes."

"I doubt that. She seems very protective of you. She even warned me not to... let me see—I think her exact words were: 'Don't go getting ideas about him. He's not interested in getting ripped off by another, money-grabbing woman.'"

"You're kidding. She actually said that to you?"

"Yes, the first night we met, right after you knocked me halfway across the patio."

"I didn't knock you halfway across the patio. I merely pushed you down into the lounge chair."

"Which was halfway across the patio from where I was standing," Lauren insisted. She could feel herself relax and her nervousness vanish. "Anyway, back to your mom. Why did she suddenly disappear from movies?"

"Actually, her story is no different from a lot of young stars of the fifties. She got too old for the parts she was type casted for. The studios simply dropped her, telling her that no one would want to see her grow old on screen."

"Oh, my goodness. No wonder she is bitter. But, was she always so hateful?"

Cody smiled. "No, she wasn't. She was loving, gentle, and kind—just like the characters she played in her movies. That's why she was so good at those roles. It

89

was who she was."

"What caused her to change? It had to be more than just the loss of movie contracts."

"My father was the director of most of her movies, and mom found out that he was ultimately responsible for her being dropped by the studio. She never forgave him for that. Eventually, he began running around with the young starlets that replaced mom as his leading ladies, and after a year, he left us. He took most of her savings and married at least three more times. That's when my mom started to change. She didn't trust anyone after that."

"I can't say that I blame her. So, how did she end up living in my condo complex? Even though she makes it sound like she's slumming, real estate prices in that area are expensive, and she owns at least four condos."

"Actually, she owns six, or rather I own six."

"You?"

"Yes. I own her condos, but she doesn't know that. She thinks they are hers. My dad left them to me. He died a very rich man, and he left his entire estate to me. Of course, it took years of battling the lawsuits of his ex-wives, but I finally was able to clear the estate. My mother knew, at the time, that dad left the condos to me, but I lied and told her that before he died, he had secretly told me that he wanted her to have them. I thought it might soften her anger a bit. But, as you are all too keenly aware, it didn't."

Lauren's salad fork was suspended in mid-air as she listened to Cody's story, and he reached over to lightly touch her chin to close her opened mouth.

"What a story," she finally muttered.

"So, you see, I'm not a heartless, bully who would knock some poor working girl halfway across the patio without feeling deep remorse."

Lauren smiled. "I never thought you were a bully—just someone who was always rushing around and too busy to smell the roses—maybe on purpose."

Cody sat back in his chair and smiled. "Please, don't tell me that you majored in psychology."

"Nope, art history with a minor in photography."

"Well, that explains why my mom says you are always taking pictures from your verandah."

It was Lauren's turn to laugh. "I swear she watches everything I do and listens to every conversation I have. But I have to admit, she's given me some sage advice albeit always wrapped in sarcasm."

"Sarcasm is her current claim to fame," said Cody.

Lauren watched as the twinkle in his eyes disappeared, and a flash of anger replaced it.

"That probably gets old," she said sympathetically. "Doesn't she have any interests, hobbies, or anything? What does she do all day?"

"She watches her old movies, exercises, and practices yoga. She is really in excellent shape. She's also an avid reader and a health food nut. I bet she'll outlive me."

"Oh, I don't know. You look like you take pretty good care of yourself, too."

"So you think I look pretty good, do you?"

"Well, before I am forced to perjure myself, I think we'd better finish up here and head for the city. I am a working girl, you know."

91

"Still being cautious and non-committal, are you? We're going to have to work on that." He motioned to the waitress for the check and smiled seductively at Lauren.

No. No. I won't fall for someone again. I won't, Lauren silently reminded herself. "I do have one more question for you," she said.

Cody opened his wallet and slipped out the prestigious, black credit card. "Yeah, what's that?"

"What did your mom mean by saying that you weren't interested in getting ripped off by another money-grabbing woman?"

"Now that's a personal question that I don't want to discuss. But, I will simply tell you that I have never walked down the aisle and that most of the women I have been involved with were more interested in my money than in me. And, like you, I have been burned by love and have pontificated that I will never fall in love again."

"How did you know about my failure at romance and my commitment to never fall in love again?" She chuckled. "That was a stupid question. I know exactly how you found out. Well, at least, we know where we both stand on that issue."

"I'm not indicating that I am still holding on to that conviction. Haven't you heard the song 'Until Love Comes Around Again' by George Strait?"

"Yes, I have heard that song."

"Really? Somehow I pictured you more as a classic music sort of person."

"Everyone pictures us as abstruse elitists, but that's a misperception," she called over her shoulder as they got up from the table. "I like all types of music. What I listen to depends on how I'm feeling at the moment."

As they were leaving the café, Nathan approached them. Lauren had noticed him sitting on the opposite side of the restaurant and was aware that he had been staring at them all through lunch.

"Dr. Livingston, I didn't expect to see you here," said Nathan directing his full attention to Cody.

"Hello, Nathan. How's your aunt?" asked Cody.

"Oh, she's fine, as always. She'll outlive both of us."

"Well, Nathan, if you'll excuse us," interrupted Lauren, "Cody is driving me into town. I want to check on a couple of paintings in the Museum's collection."

Nathan cast a threatening glance at her. "Yes, I understand that you've decided to add a few things from the collection to our upcoming exhibit. I assume you know that it was my idea to add the paintings, and I am expecting that I will be given credit for the suggestion at the Board meeting."

"No, Nathan, I wasn't aware of that. You haven't been involved with any of the planning to date, so I obviously have no idea what suggestions you have to offer or what, if any, recognition you deserve. Besides, our work on exhibitions is supposed to be a team effort. We will all be praised or blamed depending on how the exhibition is received."

"I am a team player, but I prefer to pick my team," responded Nathan leaning toward her in an obvious attempt to intimidate her, but Lauren didn't flinch and simply glared back at him. He then once again turned on his fake charm and directed his attention back to Cody. "Well, it was nice to see you again, Dr. Livingston." Then, quickly whirling around, he stormed off toward the front entrance of the museum.

"Ouch," said Cody. "I'm surprised I wasn't burned by the sparks flying between the two of you. I take it you don't get along."

"I'm sorry. I probably shouldn't have responded that way in front of you. But that man is a real thorn in my otherwise rosy work environment."

"Aren't you his boss?" asked Cody.

"Technically, I am. But, what we do is more a team effort with me being the facilitator. Only, he refuses to be facilitated. Personally, and off the record, I think he is a horrible person, and I apologize if he is a friend of yours."

"No. Actually, I don't care for him either. His aunt is a patient of mine, and I know he just wants her to die so he can have her money. Unfortunately, he's her only relative."

"Well, I hope you can keep her alive until he's too old to benefit from her estate."

Cody laughed. "You really don't like him, do you?"

As they reached the parking lot, Lauren started to open the door on the passenger's side of the Ferrari, but Cody stopped her. "Here, let me do that for you. Chivalry is not entirely dead. My mother taught me well."

"I'm sorry. I'm not used to such politeness." She turned around and smiled. His face was so close to hers that she suddenly felt a swell of passion that she knew he could see in her eyes. She quickly looked away and practically fell into the car. "Wow, this car almost sits on the ground doesn't it?" she said without daring to look at him again.

With the road and wind noise in the convertible making conversation impractical, she simply leaned her head back against the soft leather seat and let the warmth of the sun shine down on her face and the cool, California air blow through her hair. The classical music from the radio was calming and relaxing. Several times she could feel Cody looking over at her, and she returned his smile. So this is what pure pleasure feels like, she thought.

When they reached the storage facility, she remembered that Cody would not be allowed to go inside with her. New regulations that she had implemented, prevented anyone from entering the building other than curators, museum administrators, authorized conservators accompanied by curators, and Museum Board members.

"I'm sorry, Cody. But, you can't go inside with me. I'm not sure that this is public information, but we've had some theft of several paintings and, unfortunately, I implemented new regulations to limit access to the storage facility. I won't be long. I have the exact shelving and drawer locations of the pieces I want to see."

"No problem. I'll just take a quick nap while you're gone. Don't hurry. This is my day off, and I have no place I need to be, unless, of course, I get an emergency call. Then, I'll blow my horn three times. If that happens, in all likelihood, you'll have to get a cab back to the Museum."

"I understand," she called over her shoulder as she climbed the steps to the front entrance and rang the buzzer next to a large metal door. She watched as the security camera turned her direction.

"Can I help you," called a male voice over the speaker.

"Yes," answered Lauren. "I'm Lauren Allen, Head Curator of the Museum." She held up her identification badge so the security guard could see it.

The door slowly opened and a young man stepped out onto the small concrete landing. He glanced at the Ferrari below them. "Nice car," he said. "Is he with you?" he asked.

"Yes, he drove me down from the Village."

"Don't you want to let him come in out of the sun?"

"He's not authorized personnel," Lauren answered somewhat annoyed.

"Well, Mr. Nordstrom told me last week that so long as someone was with a curator, they were allowed to come in. He's always bringing in someone with him whenever he comes down here."

Lauren was stunned. She glanced down at the nametag of the security guard. "Well, James, I happen to be Nathan Nordstrom's boss, and I am here to tell you that no one other than those listed on the authorized visitor's list that I see laying on your desk is ever to step one foot in this building regardless of who is with them. Is that understood?"

"Yes, ma'am. I'm sorry. Mr. Nordstrom told me he was the boss."

Lauren fumed. "No, he isn't. He is nobody's boss, and I want you to call me immediately if he tries to bully his way around those regulations."

She handed him her business card and opened the door that led into the cavernous, temperature, light, and moisture controlled storage area. She quickly headed for the racks where the framed collections were kept. She finally reached the appropriate rack number of the print

that she wanted to see. It was another Warhol original—
not as valuable as the one that had been stolen, but
nevertheless still very valuable. She had to admit that
Nathan was right, the painting would be a perfect
addition to the new exhibition.

After staring at the painting for several minutes, she had
a strange feeling that something was not exactly right
about it. Although she had never seen the original of the
famous work, she had seen many copies of it. She was
not particularly a fan of Warhol because she felt he
violated copyright laws by using, without permission,
images of contemporary idols from magazines,
newspapers, and press photos to mass-produce copies of
the images. Among his more famous iconic prints were
those of Elizabeth Taylor, Elvis Presley, and Marilyn
Monroe. Regardless of how she felt about his
resourcefulness, she admired his success at blurring the
line between commercial art and fine art, the
interdisciplinary nature of his works, and his
contributions to contemporary art through the
introduction of new technologies such as photographic
silk-screening and new methods such as repetition and
mass production. He was among the most celebrated of
the pop artists that the Museum collected. Their Warhol
collection was one of the largest in the country thanks to
the generous donation of a wealthy patron. The museum
was indeed fortunate to have several originals of his silk
screens and paintings.

She continued to stare at the painting from various
angles. After several minutes, she carefully pulled it
away from the rack to look at the back of it, and she
immediately froze in disbelief. There was no
authentication notice on it from the Andy Warhol Art
Authentication Board.

She knew that the provenance of the Museum's painting

was from the Andy Warhol estate, so she quickly checked the canvas overlap for the confirmation by Fred Hughes, the Executor of the Estate of Andy Warhol. Hughes confirmed the authentication of all paintings by his handwritten legend on the overlap on each of them. For every painting purchased or donated from the estate, Hughes signed it and certified that it was an original painting by Andy Warhol and indicated the exact completion date of the painting. She knew that the painting she was staring at was completed in 1962, but there was no such authentication on any canvas overlap of the painting.

She suddenly felt light headed and nauseous. The room seemed to be spinning, and she quickly sat down on the cool, wooden floor to keep from falling. Afraid that she was going to faint, she leaned forward and dropped her head between her knees. "Oh, my god," she moaned.

James quickly came around the corner. "What is it, Ms. Allen? Are you ill?"

Lauren glanced up at him and tried to focus her eyes on his face. She finally muttered, "I need to see the conservator record on this painting."

"Oh, that's the painting that was cleaned by the conservator that Mr. Nordstrom always uses. He just returned this painting yesterday. It's been out being cleaned for more than a month. I understand that it's worth a lot of money."

"It used to be," she muttered. Finally, gathering her wits, she looked up at James. "Can you pull up the security video of the man who delivered this painting?"

"Sure." He reached his hand out to help Lauren up from the floor.

She followed him to the security office. She still wasn't

98

sure that she wasn't going to pass out.

James quickly located the digital video of the conservator, and Lauren leaned in close to the computer screen to get a better look. The man stood with his back to the camera. He wore a huge Panama hat and a rather expensive looking navy blue pinstriped suit. When he turned to enter the door, he dropped his head and all she could see was the brim of his hat.

"I can't tell a thing from that picture. Who is he?" she asked.

"His name is Edwin Snively." James picked up the list of authorized personnel. "See, he's right here on the bottom of the list. Mr. Nordstrom had me add him because he somehow was missed on the original list. He comes here at least twice a month with Mr. Nordstrom to pick up the paintings that Mr. Nordstrom suggests. He always brings them back good as new in a couple of weeks," answered James proudly.

I'm sure he does; brand new, she thought. "I will need for you to find out everything you have on him. I need a list of every painting he supposedly conserved, his name, address, anything you can gather. I'm going to call your boss on my way back to the Museum, but, in the meantime, you are not to let anyone in this building. I don't care who they are. Do you understand?"

"Am I in trouble? I only followed Mr. Nordstrom's instructions. I can't afford to lose my job."

"No, James, you aren't in trouble, that is, unless you let someone in the building before you call me and get clearance for them to come in. And make sure you tell the night guard, too."

"I won't let anyone in, and I'll make sure that Josh knows not to let anyone in tonight. You can count on us, but may I ask why? Is something wrong with the painting you were looking at?"

"Yes," answered Lauren. "Something is very wrong with it." She was just about to leave, when she heard Cody honk his horn three times. She went flying out the door and ran down the steps to the car. "What is it?" she asked jumping in the car with him. "Please tell me you're headed back to the Village?"

"I am," said Cody, "but I won't have time to take you as far as the Museum. I have to get to the hospital. Nathan Nordstrom's aunt was just brought into the emergency room. She's unconscious."

"Oh no," moaned Lauren reaching for her seatbelt as Cody peeled from the parking lot. "Just drop me off at the hospital. I can get someone to pick me up from there."

"You can just take the Ferrari and then pick me up later." He glanced over at her. "Is something wrong with you? You're as pale as a ghost. What happened in there?"

Lauren stared at him as the tears flooded down her cheeks. "I think Nathan Nordstrom is responsible for the theft of the art missing from the Museum's collection. And, I think that the two missing pieces that the Museum knows about are just the tip of the iceberg. Cody, this could destroy the Museum, my job, and my career."

CHAPTER 14

On the way back to the Museum, Lauren called Dr. Cromwell. Unfortunately, his phone went directly to his secretary, Virginia. "I'm sorry, Lauren, but Dr. Cromwell is in a conference and doesn't want to be disturbed. I can buzz you as soon as he is free."

"No. That's all right. I'm on my cell phone and coming back from the Museum storage facility. But, please tell him that I want to see him before he leaves for the day. It's urgent."

"Will do," said Virginia. "It seems like everything is urgent today."

Lauren ended the call. I wonder what else is going on, she thought as she dialed Crystal's number. She listened as Crystal's phone continued to ring. "Come on, Crystal, pick up the darn phone." Finally, she gave up. "Dammit," she said.

"What's wrong now?" asked Cody. "Your face has gone from ghostly white to fire engine red."

"I can't reach anyone at the Museum. I was hoping to get to Dr. Cromwell before 5:00, so we could confront Nathan before he leaves. I have this sick feeling that he intends to be long gone before I get back to the museum."

"Lauren, don't you think that this is a job for the Museum security and the police. If what you think is going on, actually is happening, you could be putting yourself in a lot of danger."

Lauren looked over at him with complete shock. "I never thought about that. Oh, my god, I should have stayed in New York."

Cody reached over and took hold of her hand. "If you'd have stayed in New York, we would never have met." He brought her hand to his lips and tenderly kissed her fingertips.

Lauren could feel her heart skip a beat and her breath leave her body. Could what I am feeling be real? After all, I have only seen Cody three times. How could I fall in love that fast? It took me a year or more before I realized that I was in love with Derrick. Derrick...my god, I haven't thought of him in days. Halleluiah, he's actually gone from my mind and my heart.

Cody let loose of her hand and smiled over at her as he flipped the radio over to the media player. He turned the volume up louder as George Strait's strong voice blasted "When love comes around again...."

As they approached the Village, he turned off the music. "Just call me when you are finished at the Museum. I'm assuming my cell number has been stored in your favorites." He smiled over at her again.

"You're certainly pretty sure of yourself," answered Lauren returning his smile.

"I am feeling confident. Your eyes have betrayed you," he said, "and I certainly haven't tried to hide my feelings. It should be obvious that, though it is happening awfully fast, I am falling in love with you."

For the remainder of the ride, they simply held each other's hands and neither of them spoke or thought about anything but the emotions that were ravaging their bodies.

When he stopped at the emergency entrance of the hospital, he leaned across the console to kiss her on the tip of her nose. "I may be a while, but you can meet me here when you're finished," he said. "And, don't go playing super hero, let the authorities take care of Nathan Nordstrom."

Lauren suddenly realized that he actually did expect her to drive his Ferrari the short distance to the Museum. "Wait, Cody. I have never driven a car like this. I'd rather jog to the Museum than risk doing something to this mechanical work of art."

Cody laughed. "Do you always see everything as a work of art? Don't worry. The car practically drives itself. You have driven a car before, haven't you?"

"Of course, but not a Ferrari. And, I don't have a California license."

"Well, then I suggest that you mind the rules of the road. Ferrari's tend to be a favorite target of Village police. See you in a bit. Be careful, and I'm not talking about taking care of the car," he warned again.

He waved and blew her a kiss as he hurried toward the entrance of the hospital. Lauren immediately got out of the car and walked around to the driver's side. As she opened the door to get in, she was aware that everyone standing outside of the hospital entrance was watching her.

"I can do this," she muttered as she glanced down at the gearshift. The car leaped forward with a jerk when she first drove away, but she smoothly shifted into second and roared out of the parking lot as if she had been driving Ferrari's all her life. "I guess there are just some things you never forget," she said aloud as a memory of her old Beatle that she drove when she was in college flashed through her mind.

When she arrived at the Museum, she was surprised to see that Nathan's car was still in the parking lot. She glanced down at her watch—4:30; not much time before he would be leaving for the day. She had been certain that he would have left before now. Surely, he didn't think that she was so dumb as to not check on the authentication of the paintings.

Hurrying up the back stairs, she knocked on Crystal's door. She turned the knob and realized that the door was locked. Glancing down at the bottom of the door, she smiled when she located the piece of tape.

She was disappointed at not being able to share her discovery with Crystal and turned around to go back to her own office. She immediately dialed Dr. Cromwell's office. Virginia answered again.

"Dr. Cromwell's office. Hello, Lauren. You're obviously back, but he's still tied up with Nathan."

"Nathan?" Lauren blurted out.

"Yes. They've been in there for more than an hour? I promise I'll call you as soon as Nathan leaves."

"Thanks." Lauren hung up the phone and turned around in her chair to stare out at the ocean. "Please work your magic and calm me down," she whispered. She jumped when her cell phone vibrated across her desk. She grabbed it and recognized the number. It was Cody.

"Hello, Cody? Are you finished already?"

"No, but I think you should know that Nathan's aunt has been poisoned."

Lauren's hands instantly turned ice cold. "Oh my god, Cody. Is she still alive?"

"Yes. I think we caught it just in time, but we won't know for sure until we determine how much damage has been done to her kidneys. Thank god her housemaid had enough sense to grab the medicine that she had been taking so we could have it analyzed right away."

"Aren't you her doctor? Wouldn't it be something that you prescribed?" Lauren was immediately sorry that she had asked the last question. "I'm sorry," she said immediately. "I didn't mean that the way it sounded."

"I know you didn't. Unfortunately, it was a medication that I had prescribed, but the capsules had been emptied and filled with some sort of strange powder. So far, the lab hasn't been able to tell what type of chemical was used to poison her. According to the housemaid, Nathan offered to pick up his aunt's prescriptions the last time they needed to be refilled. The housemaid said that Mrs. Nordstrom started feeling badly shortly after she started taking the new prescription. The police are on their way here right now. I'm sure they'll want to talk with me about the prescription, so I may be tied up for a while."

"Surely, they don't think you had anything to do with poisoning her," muttered Lauren.

"They'll have to check out everyone who had anything to do with the prescription—me, the pharmacist, even her poor housemaid and other household staff. Also, I'm sure they'll want to talk to Nathan. Regardless, I'm going to be staying here all night to monitor her progress."

"Oh my god. He's more evil than I thought." She glanced over at the desk phone when it buzzed. "I've got to take another call, Cody. I will come straight to the hospital as soon as I talk with Dr. Cromwell."

She quickly reached for the desk phone.

"Dr. Cromwell wants to see you immediately," said Virginia.

"I'm on my way," answered Lauren. As she rushed down the hallway, she passed by Nathan's office. The door was closed, but she could hear him talking on the phone. She hurried to the elevator and pushed the button for the third floor.

"Go right in," said Virginia when she entered the reception area outside of Dr. Cromwell's office.

"Have a seat, Lauren," said Dr. Cromwell coldly. "I have to say that I am disappointed in both you and Crystal."

"What? What are you talking about, Dr. Cromwell?"

"Nathan just left here. He gave me his resignation stating that he could no longer work under such uncomfortable and unprofessional circumstances. He has filed a claim of harassment against you and Crystal."

"Whatever Nathan has told you, it's a lie," said Lauren jumping up and leaning over the massive desk. "I can prove it," she shouted.

"I hope you can," he said. "Because if you can't, I will be forced to let both you and Crystal go."

Dr. Cromwell's cell phone rang, and he glanced at the name on caller ID. He looked over at her with a deep scowl on his face. "It's one of our most valuable patrons. I have to take this."

Lauren started to leave, but he motioned for her to sit back down.

"Hello, Mrs. Dennison. How can I help you?"

Lauren watched as Dr. Cromwell's face transitioned from pale to flush and back to pale.

106

"I know," he said. "He's a very important part of the Museum. Believe me I am doing everything I can to make him change his mind."

There was a momentary pause and Lauren could hear the animated voice of a woman practically shouting on the phone.

"I understand," said Dr. Cromwell. "I'll keep you abreast of the situation." He hung up the phone and glared at her across his desk.

"Let me guess," said Lauren. "Nathan called her and probably all the other major donors to tell them that he was being forced to resign."

Dr. Cromwell's phone rang again. "It's another of our major patrons," he said sighing.

"I'll be right back," said Lauren jumping up from her chair and running from the room.

She immediately headed for her office to retrieve her cell phone. As she turned the corner, she noticed that her office door was opened. She knew she had closed it before she had left, and she instantly regretted that she hadn't taken the time to lock it. When she rushed into the room, she stared at the empty spot on her desk where she had left her now missing cell phone.

Furious, she headed straight to Nathan's office. She burst through the open door, but the office was empty. She whipped around and headed back to her office to see if Crystal had emailed her the video. As she came around the desk, she glanced out the window at the parking lot below, attempting to see if Nathan's car was still in the parking lot. He couldn't have been gone very long, she thought. She was immediately surprised to see a black sedan pull into the driveway and block Nathan's car. Two burly looking men jumped from the back seat of the

107

sedan and pulled Nathan from his car. Nathan tried to break their hold on him, but they overpowered him and shoved him into the back seat of the large, black sedan. The man driving the sedan was wearing a huge Panama hat. "So that's Edwin Snively," she said. When he looked up at her, she quickly stepped away from the window.

For several moments, she was paralyzed with fear. What if they come up the back stairs and drag me away too? She held her breath until she heard the squeal of the tires as they pulled out of the Museum driveway. Once she was sure they were gone, she quickly stepped back up toward the window, hoping she could get a look at the license plate on the sedan, but she was too late. The sedan was already at the corner and too far away for her to make out the numbers on the license plate. As she watched the sedan pull out into traffic, she noticed a black van parked across the street from the museum parking lot quickly make a U-turn and head for the corner. She could have sworn that she saw Crystal driving the van.

Her desk phone buzzed again, and she quickly grabbed it. "Dr. Cromwell, I think Nathan is in trouble. I just saw him being taken away by two men in a black sedan. I'm on my way back to your office, and I think you should call the police."

She hung up the phone and raced back into Dr. Cromwell's office. "Did you contact the police? Is David Mesa still here?" Without giving him a chance to respond she blurted out what she had seen at the Museum storage facility. "I think that we've only seen the tip of the iceberg of the number of missing paintings," she said as she plopped down in the nearest chair.

Dr. Cromwell sat in stunned silence simply staring at her

with his eyes glazed over as if he had gone into shock or something. She waited for him to say something, but it didn't appear that he was capable of uttering a word. Finally, she asked again, "Have you already notified the police? If not, I think we should call them immediately."

He appeared to suddenly snap out of his stupor and quickly reached for the phone to make a call. "Dale," he said.

Lauren recognized the first name of the Chairman of the Museum Board. "What?" she blurted out. "What can he do to help us?"

Dr. Cromwell stuck his hand out as an indication for her to be patient. She got up and paced back and forth in front of his desk, occasionally glancing angrily at him. He was just sitting there in stunned silence, listening while the voice on the other end seemed to drone on and on. Several times he looked over at her and shook his head. When he finally hung up the phone, he got up and came around the desk to where she was standing with her arms folded across her chest and her foot angrily tapping on the floor.

He held his hand out to her and calmly said, "I apologize for not standing up for you and Crystal when I spoke to Nathan. I should have known that he was lying, but he indicated that he had a video to substantiate his claim."

"Crystal and I are the ones with the video, although since my cell phone and Crystal have both suddenly disappeared, I can't produce it."

"Never mind the video. I believe you, but, unfortunately, what we need to do right now is to go back to the Museum storage facility. I need for you to help me inventory the lost paintings that Nathan has stolen."

109

"So I was right about him?"

"Yes. Evidently it has been going on for several months."

"Aren't you going to call the police? As much as I don't like or respect Nathan and even if he is a thief, I still think he is in trouble and needs help. I think the thugs that he's mixed up with are dangerous."

"Nathan has obviously dug his own hole. Right now, our task is to find out what has been stolen. I've just been made aware that others are tracking down the criminals." He went back around his desk and shut down his computer.

"Do you need to get anything from your office?" he asked.

"Yes, and I have to drop off a friend's car at the hospital on our way back to the storage facility. Do you mind following me over there?"

"No, of course not. That's the least I can do," he responded.

CHAPTER 15

Lauren approached the information desk at the hospital.

"May I help you," greeted the pretty, white-haired volunteer seated at the desk.

"I'm Lauren Allen. I'm here to see Dr. Cody Livingston," responded Lauren. "He's somewhere in the hospital with a patient by the name of Mrs. Nordstrom."

The woman typed in the name and reached for the telephone to dial an extension. "Dr. Livingston, there is a Miss Lauren Allen in the lobby to see you. Ok, I'll send her right up."

She smiled up at Lauren. "He said to send you up to the patient's room. It's on the fifth floor, room 512. Visitor elevators are straight down that hall," she said pointing to a doorway to the left of the reception desk.

Lauren was still nervous about everything she had seen at the Museum and somewhat frustrated because Dr. Cromwell refused to explain why he wouldn't call the police or why Crystal had suddenly disappeared.

Cody met her at the elevator when she reached the fifth floor. The minute she saw him tears flowed down her cheeks.

"Lauren, what is it? Did you wreck the Ferrari?" he asked, half in jest.

"I wish that was all that was wrong," she said.

Cody reached out and pulled her into his arms. "Then, what is it? You look utterly miserable." Noticing that the nurses were watching them, he added, "Come on, let's go into Mrs. Nordstrom's room, and you can tell me all about it. We'll have some privacy there."

"I don't have much time. Dr. Cromwell is waiting to take me back to the storage facility. We'll probably be there half of the night."

"You're going back there again? Why?" he asked as he led her down the hall.

As they walked into Mrs. Nordstrom's room, Lauren suddenly stopped and gasped. She stared at the women lying in the hospital bed as if she couldn't believe her eyes.

"What is it?" asked Cody. "Don't be alarmed. She's not dead; she's just sleeping."

"Oh, my goodness, Cody. I know her."

The sound of voices in the room caused Mary Nordstrom's eyes to flutter and finally open. For a moment, she stared at Lauren obviously trying to understand why she looked so familiar. Suddenly, a big smile came across her face. "I've missed seeing you," she muttered.

Lauren rushed to her bedside and gently took hold of her hand. "I've missed you, too. How are you, and how's Rochester taking all of this?"

"You two know one another?" asked Cody. "How? Through the Museum?"

Mary quickly turned to look at Lauren. "Do you work at the Museum? Then, you must know my hateful nephew, Nathan Nordstrom."

Lauren hesitated a moment trying to decide if she should disclose what she knew about Nathan's possible abduction. She decided against it. "I'm afraid I do," she said.

"He tried to kill me, you know. The police are looking for him as we speak, but he seems to have disappeared. Thanks to Dr. Livingston, he didn't get my inheritance, and I am making sure that he never does. I'm changing my will in the morning. I'm considering leaving everything to Rochester."

Lauren looked over at Cody, who rolled his eyes and shook his head. "You might want to reconsider that," said Lauren. "Rochester looks like he's getting up there in age, and you look as spry as ever."

"Thanks to Dr. Livingston," Mary repeated. "But, you know, aside from my house staff, Rochester is the only family I have left." She reached out and grabbed hold of Lauren's hand. "My husband and I took Nathan in after his parents were killed in an automobile wreck. We raised him like he was our own, but no matter what we did for him, it never seemed to be enough. I think he felt that the world owed him something because he lost his parents."

"Did you have other children?" asked Lauren, who was deeply touched by the sadness in Mary's eyes.

"No, I could never have children." Mary reached up and touched Lauren's face. "I always wanted to have a daughter like you." She gently patted Lauren on the cheek. "But, I guess it was never meant to be, and now I'm an old lady with only a stubborn, aging English Terrier to love."

Suddenly, Betsy Hannah's situation flashed through Lauren's mind. She grabbed hold of Mary's hand. "Did you every meet Betsy Hannah, Nathan's friend?"

"Yes. I met her several times. Nathan often brought her

by the house. She is a delightful young woman, and, frankly, I never could figure out what she saw in him."

Lauren drew in a long breath, she wasn't sure that what she was about to suggest was wise. "I hope I am not giving you false hopes, but did you know that Betsy gave birth three months ago to a baby girl?"

Mary stared at her in amazement. "No, I didn't know. Do you know who the baby's father is?"

"Honestly, I don't, but I have a strong suspicion that it might be Nathan. In spite of all of his faults, Betsy is madly in love with him."

Mary stared at her for a long time without saying a word. Finally she whispered, "Could it be that I do have another relative after all? Wouldn't that be something— and a little girl to boot? When I get out of this hospital, I'm going to check all this out. I bet that young lady is struggling and could use some help. I doubt that Nathan has offered any assistance whether or not he knew about the baby. He's too self-serving to do anything respectful like that." She smiled and reached out her arms to Lauren. "You have given this old woman something to hope for, and even if it turns out that Nathan's not the father, I like Betsy, and I'm going to check in on her."

Cody smiled at Lauren and leaned over and whispered in her ear. "She needed something to hang on to. Thanks," He then turned to Mary. "Hey, you still haven't explained how you two know each other," he said.

"Like Romeo and Juliet," said Mary. "I met her every morning under her balcony."

Lauren laughed. She knew she would like her verandah friend, once she got a chance to actually meet her. "I'm Lauren Allen, by the way," she said to Mary. "And, you aren't going to believe this, but I thought you looked like a Mary the first time I saw you. That was the imaginary name I gave you."

Mary smiled. "Well, I called you Elizabeth because you looked like you should be a queen."

"That's odd," said Lauren. "That's the name that Rex gave me, too."

"Who?" asked Mary.

Cody exhaled a long sigh. "Ok, now I am confused. Who is Rex?"

Lauren reached out and took his hand. "Actually, that was his stage name. His real name is Dan."

Cody plopped down in a straight back chair next to Mary and turned around to look up at Lauren. "What?" he asked obviously bewildered by the entire conversation.

"He's another of my balcony friends. Mary, I bet you've seen him. He rides the strange looking tricycle down the street every morning."

"Yes, I have noticed him. He moves so slowly that I often wonder if he makes it back to wherever he started from before the sun sets."

Lauren laughed again and then suddenly turned toward the door. "Oh, my gosh, I almost forgot. Dr. Cromwell is waiting for me. I've got to go." She quickly leaned over and kissed Cody on the cheek. Then realizing what she had spontaneously done, she looked at him with complete embarrassment. "Is it all right that I just did that?" she asked.

Cody reached out and grabbed her hand. "Why wouldn't it be?" he asked.

"Isn't this nice," said Mary. "My two favorite people are

115

in love with each other. You see, Lauren, this is another of those moments that I was telling you about that makes you glad to be alive."

Lauren reached across the bed and gave Mary a gentle hug. "It certainly is," she whispered in Mary's ear.

Cody followed her out into the hall "You still haven't told me what was upsetting you," he said.

"I didn't want to say anything in front of Mary, but from my office window, I saw two men grab Nathan and force him into the back of a black sedan. I tried to get Dr. Cromwell to call the police, but he said that the authorities were tracking the criminals and that what we needed to do was to get an inventory of all the missing paintings. So, that's why we are going back to the storage facility. I'm not used to all this cloak and dagger stuff. And, I admit that I'm a little unnerved by it all."

"Lauren, I don't want you to go back there. Let me call the police," said Cody pulling her into his arms. "Please, don't go."

"I have to," she said. "I'm sure I'll be fine. I just got a little frightened when I saw them force Nathan into their car. There's security at the storage facility, and I'm sure Dr. Cromwell will make sure that I get home all right."

"Call me when you leave the storage facility, and I'll meet you at your condo to make sure you are tucked in safe and sound."

"Darn it," she said. "I can't call you. Nathan stole my cell phone."

"What?"

"Don't worry. I'm a big girl, and I've been tucking myself in for a long time."

"Well, I'm sure you would enjoy it more, if I did it," he said as he pulled her into his arms and kissed her longingly on the lips.

Lauren smiled up at him. "Maybe it would be better if you tucked me in."

As she stepped onto the elevator, she suddenly stuck her hand out to stop the door from closing. "I almost forgot." She reached in her purse and pulled out the keys to the Ferrari. "You'll probably need these," she said as she tossed them to him.

"Not to worry," he said. "I always have a spare set, but be careful. I still don't like the idea of you going back there, especially at night."

"Thanks for worrying about me," she called as the elevator door slid shut.

CHAPTER 16

It was after one o'clock when Dr. Cromwell turned onto the street that led to Lauren's condo. They had spent an emotionally draining seven hours painstakingly examining each piece of the framed art in the main collection. More than twenty pieces were either missing altogether or had been copied. It was obvious that Nathan had been selling off the Collection for quite some time.

As he started to stop in front of her condo, Lauren noticed the black sedan parked across the street. "Oh my god, Dr. Cromwell, don't stop. Keep going."

"What is it?" he asked as he accelerated past the condo entrance.

"That black sedan across the street—it looks like the one that Nathan was abducted in."

"How would they know where you lived, and why would they be waiting for you?"

Lauren scooted down in the seat as they passed the sedan. "I saw them from my window at the office, and the driver noticed that I was watching the whole thing," said Lauren.

"But how would they know where you lived?"

"I don't know. I think Nathan stole my cell phone. I put my address on the back of the cover in case I lost it, so someone could return it to me. Obviously, that wasn't a smart thing to do."

"What do you want me to do?" asked Dr. Cromwell. "I

can't call the police, yet."

"I don't understand that," Lauren said. "Why don't you want to involve the police?"

"I can't tell you that, right now. Just be assured that there is work being done to capture the criminals working with Nathan. As soon as he leads them to the mastermind of the theft, I'm certain that they'll move in and arrest them all. We'll stand a better chance of recovering the stolen art if we don't involve the police right now."

"Is Crystal somehow involved in all of this?"

Dr. Cromwell shifted uncomfortably in his seat. "I'd rather not answer that right now either."

"She is. I know it." Lauren glanced in the side mirror to see if anyone was behind them. "It doesn't appear that the sedan followed us, so you can pull over here, and I'll go in the back entrance of the condo." She gathered up her purse and notes as Dr. Cromwell pulled to the curb.

"Are you sure you'll be safe getting out here?" he asked.

"I'm sure. I don't have to go far to get to the back entrance." Lauren quickly got out of the car and ran up the back stairs to the locked, rear gate of the condos. In the darkness, she fumbled for her keys and finally found the right one. As she turned the key, she heard footsteps behind her. She quickly opened the gate and hurriedly tried to get inside. Just as she was about to get the gate closed, someone crashed against it knocking her to the ground.

When she looked up, she was staring into the malicious eyes of Edwin Snively. He grabbed her by the arm and pulled her up from the ground swinging her around.

"Scream and I'll shoot you on the spot," he snarled

sticking a gun in her face.

"What do you want from me?" she said yanking on her arm and trying to sound brave.

"You are going to take us to the Museum storage facility," he snarled. "Apparently, you are the only one that your security will open the door for."

He dragged her back down the steps to where the black sedan was waiting. Two men got out of the back seat, grabbed her by the arm, and shoved her into the car.

As they drove away from the condo, Lauren noticed the black van parked across the street. She prayed that whoever was inside of it would follow them.

CHAPTER 17

Crystal watched through the tinted windows of the van as Lauren was forced into the back seat of the sedan. "Darn it," she said. "I was afraid of this."

She waited several minutes until the sedan had turned the corner before she made a U-turn and slowly approached the intersection. She wanted to make sure there was other traffic between the van and the sedan, and at this time of night in the Village, there wasn't much traffic.

"Where do you think they're headed?" asked Jake.

"My guess is that they're going to the Museum storage facility. They must not have gotten everything they wanted before Lauren put an end to Nathan's access to it."

"If you're sure that's where they're going, why don't you just take a different route rather than risk the chance that they'll spot us," asked Jake

"I would if I were certain that's where they're headed. Since they dumped Nathan off at that old warehouse, we've lost our GPS connection, so now I can't afford to lose them in case I'm wrong. But, I am worried that they may pick up our tag this late at night."

"You'll be all right as soon as you hit I-5, there's always plenty of traffic on the interstate."

Crystal slowed the van to allow a couple of cars to pass her. She was worried about Lauren and didn't want to do anything to jeopardize their chance to rescue her.

She'll be all right until they get inside, she thought. But once they go in, I'm not sure what they might do. "If it appears that Lauren might be in physical danger, I intend to end all of this at the Museum's storage facility," she said turning toward Jake.

"Your old man wouldn't want you to do that, you know it. We have to get the paintings back; that's what we are hired to do. Have you forgotten his most important rule? Never let your feelings about the client prevent you from doing what you're assigned to do. Remember?"

Crystal looked over and frowned at him. "Lauren is not a client. She is an innocent bystander who just got caught up in this mess."

"But she did get caught up in it, and our job is to recover the stolen paintings. We weren't hired to protect your friend."

"How can you be so heartless? I know my dad would agree with me."

"Have you ever been on assignment with your dad?" asked Jake.

"No. He refuses to let me get involved in his cases."

"Well, I've worked with him numerous times. And, believe me, he sticks to that rule regardless of who gets in the way."

Crystal looked over at Jake with disbelief. She couldn't imagine her dad not agreeing with her intention to save Lauren. Surely, he would want her to protect her. Suddenly, she remembered his words from this morning. 'Lauren is not your concern,' he had said. "Oh, my god," she blurted out.

"What is it?" asked Jake.

"Never mind," she said.

She changed lanes as she noticed that the sedan was exiting onto East Genesee Avenue. "I knew it. That's the exit for the Museum storage facility," she said. To make sure that the driver in the sedan didn't suspect that they were following him, she intentionally drove past the exit and then made a sudden U-turn at the first emergency opening on the highway.

Jake braced himself against the passenger door to avoid hitting his head on the window. "You could have warned me that you intended to do a flip-flop like that," he shouted. "And, of course, you knew that it was illegal to make a U-turn back there. That break in the dividers is for emergency vehicles only."

"This is an emergency," responded Crystal stomping on the accelerator and dodging in and out and around the other cars on the freeway.

She finally turned on the west exit of Genesee and did another immediate U-turn to head east toward the Museum storage facility. She turned off the lights and coasted to a used car lot across the street where she could still see the entrance of the building.

She saw Lauren standing alone on the landing of the front entrance. The others were crouched close to a wall behind the landing so that the camera couldn't see them.

The moment the door opened, two of the men stormed up the stairs and shoved Lauren through the door ahead of them. The third man pulled a gun and shot through the lens of the security camera as he pulled the door shut.

"Now we wait," said Jake. "And, we know that they are armed."

"You didn't really think they wouldn't be, did you? I'm

going in," said Crystal opening her door.

Jake grabbed her by the arm and pulled her back inside. "No, you're not," said Jake. "There are three of them, and there is no way in there but through that closed door. Be sensible, Crystal. There is nothing you can do except pray that they won't kill her."

"Oh, my god, how can I ever live with myself?" She dropped her head against the steering wheel and covered her ears. If there were shots fired, she didn't want to hear them.

After several minutes, the door opened again, and two men came out carrying several small paintings. They opened the trunk of the car and put the paintings inside.

"At least they won't put her in the trunk when they bring her back out," Crystal whispered.

"You mean *if* they bring her out," answered Jake.

Crystal whirled around and stared at him. "Don't say that. Maybe they'll take her back to the abandoned warehouse where the left Nathan thinking they'll get rid of her and Nathan at the same place. I can then have another chance to save her," she said.

"Here they come," answered Jake. "It looks like they are going to take her and the security guard with them. That doesn't make any sense to me."

"Get down," said Crystal as the sedan's headlights flashed past the van. She held her breath until she saw the taillights of the sedan through the front window.

"Let's go," said Jake.

Crystal waited until after the sedan had turned the corner before starting the engine. "They obviously have used the abandoned warehouse to store the paintings they

124

have stolen, and now they must have all they want, so they're going to move them out to be shipped to god knows where. You'd better warn Tom, that they're headed his way."

"He texted me just a minute ago that a large moving van had just pulled out of the old warehouse. "I think you're right. The paintings were being stored there."

"Of course," said Crystal. "They obviously have stored them in that moving van that has no doubt been set up to control the heat and humidity that is required to preserve the art. The paintings that they just picked up must be the last of the collection that they needed. Did he say anything about seeing Nathan?"

"No, he hasn't seen him since they first dragged him into the warehouse," said Jake. "But, I doubt that they will leave behind any hostages who could identify them," he softly added.

Crystal turned around and stared at him. "I know that," she quietly whispered. Suddenly, she stomped on the accelerator and swerved into another lane.

"What the heck are you doing?" yelled Jake.

This time I know exactly where they're going, and I intend to get there first," she yelled.

CHAPTER 18

Barbara Livingston fumbled around in the dark to find the phone next to her bed. "Who could be calling me at this hour?" she groaned. She glanced at the small screen on the hand phone and quickly pushed the speaker button. "What is it, Cody? Are you all right?"

"I'm really sorry to call at this hour, Mom. I have been trying to get hold of Lauren at her condo, but there's no answer."

"So that's been you ringing her phone off the wall. It's been driving me nuts. I had to go into the bedroom to watch TV to get away from that incessant ringing."

Cody sighed. "Look, Mom, I need you to go over and pound on her door to see if she's there. Maybe she's just a deep sleeper and doesn't hear the phone."

Mrs. Livingston glanced at the clock again. "It's two o'clock in the morning for Pete's sake. I'll wake the entire complex if I pound on her door. Someone already woke me up making a commotion outside a little while ago. I've had a terrible time getting back to sleep. I'll be awake the rest of the night if I turn on all my lights and go outside in the cool night air."

Cody shook the phone in his hand. "Mom, for once in your life, would you please think about someone else other than yourself. What kind of a commotion did you hear and when?"

"Hang on," said Mrs. Livingston, "I'm headed over to Lauren's."

Cody began pacing back and forth as he heard his

126

mother open her door and lightly knock on Lauren's. "For heaven's sake," he yelled in the phone, "no one could hear that light tap. Pound on the door."

"I will not pound on the door," said his mother. "Wait, there's a note stuck to her door. She must not have gotten home yet, or she would have taken the note in with her. Isn't it awfully late for her to be out running around? She's never been out this late before."

"Read the note, Mom, now," shouted Cody.

"I can't read someone else's mail. It's illegal."

Cody held the phone up in the air and waved it around like he was going to toss it at someone. "It isn't mail, dammit. Read it."

"Well, if you insist, but you're going to tell her that you made me read it."

"Just read the darn note."

"I can't see what it says out here. Wait a minute. I'm going back inside."

Cody took in a deep breath and bent over from the waist. He straightened up and ran his hands angrily through his hair. "Oh my god, I'm going to kill her," he muttered.

"Okay, I can see it now. Oh my goodness," she said.

"If you don't tell me what it says on that note, I swear I'm going to jump through this phone and strangle you."

"I don't think you're going to like what it says," said Mrs. Livingston.

"Mom!"

Mrs. Livingston held the phone away from her ear. "It's from someone named Crystal, and it says, "You are in danger. Stay inside."

Cody collapsed in the nearest chair and tossed the phone across the desk of the nurse's station.

"Are you all right, Dr. Livingston?" asked the night duty nurse.

He immediately picked up another phone and dialed the police.

CHAPTER 19

As soon as she approached the abandoned warehouse, Crystal pulled to the side of the road and jumped out of the van. "Keep moving, so they won't see you," she yelled at Jake.

Jake hurriedly climbed into the driver's seat. "You're insane," he shouted as he drove away. He watched in the rear view mirror as Crystal ran toward the back of the old warehouse. He turned into the next driveway and hid the van behind another abandoned building just as the black sedan pulled onto the street. Flipping off the headlights, he turned the van around so that he could see the truck parked in the drive of the old warehouse across the street.

He was trying to decide what he should do, when someone tapped on the passenger window. He immediately reached for his gun.

"Don't shoot for god's sake. It's me," whispered Tom.

"Don't do that," Jake shouted. "I could have blown your head off sneaking up on me like that. You know better than that. Am I the only one sticking to protocol around here?"

"What the heck is going on? I saw Crystal running through the weeds to the back of the building," said Tom.

"She's got it in her crazy head that she's going to save her friend from being killed."

"What happened to rule number one?" asked Tom.

"I tried to talk some sense into her, but you can see how well she listened. She's just like her old man, stubborn as a damned mule."

"How does she intend to pull that off and still get the art?"

"Don't ask me, ask her—if we ever see her again."

"We can't just sit here? If she gets so much as a scratch on her, you can bet you and I will be looking for another job," said Tom.

Jake glared at him. It wasn't his job he was worrying about. It was Crystal. Although he had tried to convince himself that he wasn't in love with her, he hadn't been able to make his heart believe it.

Their lives were worlds apart. She was from an extremely wealthy family, and he was from the other side of the tracks. She had a Masters degree from a prestigious university; he had a two-year degree in Fine Arts from a local community college. He was also ten years older than Crystal, and he was certain that he was not the husband that her parents had in mind for her. But even more important, he always got mixed signals from her about how she felt about him. Unfortunately, none of that had helped him extinguish his feelings for her. He simply couldn't help himself; he had loved her from afar since he first went to work for her father. She had still been a young college student at that time, barely out of high school.

"Here comes the sedan," whispered Tom.

"Just sit tight. I want to wait to see what they do first so I won't get in the way of Crystal's plan."

"You think she has a plan?" said Tom.

"She always has a plan—they don't always work out, but she always has a plan."

They waited in silence as the sedan slowly pulled into the driveway of the abandoned building. A man sauntered out of the ramshackle warehouse and opened the tailgate of the large truck.

Edward Snively quickly got out of the driver's seat of the sedan and opened the trunk. Carefully, he lifted out one of the paintings and carried it up the ramp of the truck.

One of his henchmen got out of the front passenger seat of the sedan, and the other one opened the back door and stood with a gun pointing at the two hostages who remained in the back seat.

"I don't get why these idiots steal famous works of art. They can never sell it at Christie's or Sotheby's where the real money exchanges hands in the art world, and buyers can't openly display or brag about owning it without the probability of being charged with receiving stolen property," muttered Tom.

Jake looked over at him and shook his head. "You are aware that the black market provides a huge venue for dumping stolen art at ridiculously high prices, right? The thieves also can try to collect large sums of ransom money from museums, art owners, and insurance companies."

"Of course I know all that, but I still don't get it. It's not like stealing diamonds or other raw gems that can't be as easily identified."

Jake exhaled an exasperated sigh. "Let's just focus on the task at hand here and stop worrying about how these jerks intend to get rich from their thefts." He continued to worry about the danger that he had allowed Crystal to put herself in rather than to think about anything or anyone else.

After Snively had moved both paintings into the truck, he walked over to the sedan, and they saw him toss his head toward the warehouse. Immediately, the two men reached into the back seat and dragged the hostages out of the car. Lauren kicked at her captor and struck out at him unsuccessfully trying to free herself.

"She's got spunk," whispered Tom.

"Yeah, like someone else we know, but it's not doing her much good."

While the two men continued to drag their struggling hostages inside, Snively and the driver got into the truck and pulled out of the driveway. They stopped at the end of the alley as if they were waiting for something or someone.

Within seconds, the two men who had taken the hostages inside burst out of the warehouse. They ran toward the sedan and practically dove into the front seats. The driver speedily backed out of the driveway before the man on the passenger side even had time to close his front door. Tom and Jake watched as the sedan squealed away from the warehouse and down the alley toward the moving van.

"What? That's it? I didn't hear any gunshots, did you?" asked Tom.

"Oh, my god," yelled Jake. He jumped out of the van and onto the ground just as an enormous explosion inside the warehouse sent debris and balls of fire spewing toward the sky. "Follow that truck and call for emergency help for here," he yelled as he ran toward the explosion. "I mean it. Stay on that truck."

CHAPTER 20

Crystal sat up and tried to move her arms and legs. Her body felt like it had been run over by a freight train, and there was a stream of blood running down her face from somewhere on top of her head. She was surrounded by broken pieces of glass and charred bricks.

She shook her head trying to remember where she was and what had happened. The last thing she remembered was crawling along the damp concrete floor of the dilapidated warehouse, and then suddenly being lifted from the ground and slammed against the back wall. The force catapulted her through the air like a rag doll. The blow when she hit the wall knocked the wind out of her and, for a moment, she just lay in a crumpled heap confused and dazed.

Suddenly realizing what was going on, she forced herself up from the ground. "Lauren," she yelled and immediately jumped back against the wall as a blazing rafter fell from above her. She glanced up at the starlight and noticed that what remained of the roof was ablaze.

"Lauren," she screamed again.

"Over here," answered a male voice. "Help me, please," he begged. "I can't move."

Crystal immediately recognized Nathan's voice. She hesitated a moment and then finally called out to him, "Keep talking, so I can find you. I can't see anything in this smoke."

Crawling along the concrete floor so she could stay below the smoke, she scrambled across the room toward Nathan's voice.

"Over here," he yelled. "I can see you."

Crystal groped through the darkness until she finally felt a foot that was sticking out from under a pile of bricks. She immediately began tossing the bricks off Nathan's legs.

"Thank god," he moaned. "I was sure I was going to die in this rat invested inferno. "I've been locked in what is left of this closet all night."

"You deserve to be locked up," said Crystal. She dug in her pocket for her knife and crawled behind Nathan to cut the electrical tape wrapped around his wrists. "There," she said. "Now come on. We have to find Lauren."

"No way," he said. "Save yourself. What's left of the roof is going to fall down any second. I'm out of here."

"For god's sake, Nathan, be a man for once in your life," she said as she watched him limp toward the back door. "Once a jerk, always a jerk," she screamed. She immediately crawled toward the front of the warehouse.

In the dense smoke, she could see a silhouette of a man running through the fire that surrounded the now missing, front doors of the warehouse. Fearing that it was one of the thieves returning to verify that the fire had accomplished what they intended, she reached for her gun.

"Crystal," yelled Jake.

"Over here, Jake. My god, I almost shot you," she answered relieved to hear his voice.

"The rest of the roof is going to come crashing down on our heads any minute. Have you found Lauren and the security guard?" said Jake.

"No, but they shoved them into a small office over there to your left and locked them in. I was headed toward them when the explosion went off."

In the distance they could hear sirens coming their way. "Good," said Jake, "Help is on the way, thanks to Tom."

"Lauren," called Crystal again, but there was no answer.

"I see them—over there," said Jake pointing toward what once must have been a glass enclosed office.

Crystal stood up and rushed toward the two bodies that were lying motionless on the ground, surrounded by broken glass and burning debris.

"Watch out," yelled Jake shoving her from behind. A huge rafter fell and landed with a horrible thud across the back of Jake's legs, pinning him to the ground face down. He frantically tried to move his legs from under the burning rafter, but he couldn't move. Crystal quickly ripped off her jacket and beat at the flames.

Outside she could see the flashing lights of several emergency vehicles as they roared to a stop. "Help, help," she screamed as she continued to use her jacket to beat out the flames that were now surrounding both her and Jake.

Within seconds that seemed like hours, two firemen rushed into the burning warehouse and blasted the flames surrounding them with a huge stream of water. She tried desperately to lift the rafter off Jakes legs.

"Get out of here, Crystal," yelled Jake. "Please, get out of here. The whole roof is going to come down any minute."

135

"I am not leaving you," she yelled. Suddenly, two more firemen appeared and easily lifted and tossed the burning rafter off Jake. One of them bent down and lifted him, tossing him over his shoulder. The other one grabbed Crystal around the waist and also headed for the front door. "No, no," she screamed. She twisted free from her would be rescuer. "My friends are still in there," she said, rushing back into the flaming building to where Lauren and the security guard were still lying on the floor. She grabbed hold of Lauren's arm, threw it across her shoulders, and began dragging her limp body toward the front door. A fireman rushed to help her and another one pushed past her to grab the security guard. As they reached the front door, they heard a thunderous crash behind them, and a sudden burst of hot air and debris propelled them forward, knocking them to the ground.

Crystal scrambled to her feet and whirled around to look back at the warehouse. The roof was completely gone, and nothing but the three exterior walls of the building was left standing. The entire structure was engulfed in huge, blistering flames that shot high above the remaining walls creating a blazing barricade of yellow, orange, and red in front of them.

She stared in horror at the scene around her. Several teams of paramedics were frantically administering to Jake, Lauren, and the security guard. Police cars were coming from different directions with sirens blaring and flashing lights lighting up the night sky. The heat from the burning building was stifling.

Someone touched her arm, causing her to jerk it away.

"Sorry, I didn't mean to startle you," said the paramedic. "I think you need to let us check you out. Those burns on your hands look like they need some attention."

She stared at him and tried to make sense out of what he was saying. Suddenly, she noticed that Jake was being lifted inside of one of the emergency vehicles. "Wait," she yelled. "I'm going with him."

She climbed into the ambulance and leaned over close to Jake. He was lying face down and motionless on the small gurney; his eyes were shut and the muscles in his face were tight and drawn. Obviously, he was desperately trying to refrain from screaming out with pain from the deep burns and crushed bones in both of his legs.

"I'm sorry, Miss. But you'll need to give us room to work on him. He's in shock and his vitals are dropping."

Crystal immediately moved out of the way. "Don't you dare leave me, Jake Cromley. I love you, you big dope," she called.

"I've loved you longer," he whispered

.

CHAPTER 21

Betsy stared at the scene on the television of a massive fire at an abandoned warehouse downtown. She pushed the reverse button several times on the controller and leaned closer to the TV set to try to get a better view of a woman who was running toward an ambulance. She was certain that the woman was Crystal Carter. Why would Crystal be at an old warehouse, she wondered.

She had been pacing around her tiny apartment all night, waiting and hoping to get a call from Nathan. She had left the Museum after lunch with a migraine, and he had promised he would come over this evening to let her explain why she had given Lauren their copies of the layout. She knew he was furious with her, and she hadn't explained what triggered her sudden decision. She didn't tell him that she had seen the video of him this morning with Crystal, but she intended to show it to him tonight since Crystal had airdropped her a copy of it to her phone this morning.

A cry from the nursery sent her running to Maria. She leaned over, picked her up, and stood there in the dark swaying back and forth. "It's okay, sweetie." she soothed. After several minutes, the baby went back to sleep, and she laid her gently back into the crib. She lingered there several minutes staring down at her beautiful daughter. "Your daddy doesn't know what he's missing by shutting you out or his life," she softly whispered.

She froze in place as the voice of a TV reporter suddenly penetrated her thoughts. She whirled around and ran back into the living room. She stared in shock as a picture of Nathan flashed on the screen, and the words "Nephew Poisons Wealthy Aunt," scrolled below it.

"No, no," she cried out. "That can't be true." She tried to concentrate on what the reporter was saying, but nothing made sense to her. She reached for her phone and frantically dialed Nathan's number. After letting it ring for what seemed forever, she finally hung up.

She turned up the volume on the TV and heard the reporter say, "Mr. Nordstrom still remains at large, but a massive search is being carried out to find him. His car was found at his place of employment, but there was no trace of Mr. Nordstrom."

"That doesn't make sense," she said. "Why would Nathan do such a horrible thing? His aunt is such a sweet person."

Her phone rang, and she quickly grabbed it. She stared at the small, black screen but didn't recognize the number.

"Hello," she said.

"Betsy, you've got to help me," whispered Nathan.

"Nathan, where are you? What's going on? The TV reported that you tried to poison your aunt. The police are looking for you."

"Betsy, stop talking and listen to me," he shouted. "I need you to come and pick me up."

A loud knock on the door of her apartment woke Maria who began loudly crying.

"Nathan, someone is at the door, and Maria is crying. I have to go."

"Don't answer the door," Nathan insisted. "It's probably the police."

Betsy got up and ran to Maria's room carrying the phone with her. The pounding on the door got louder. "Nathan, I have to answer the door."

"Okay, but don't tell them you've talked to me."

"Where are you?" she asked again.

"Call me back on the number that registered on your phone," he said and hung up.

She tossed her phone down on Maria's bed and hurried to answer the door. "Who is it?" she asked before opening it.

"Police. We have a warrant to search your apartment."

Betsy quickly opened the door. "I don't understand," she said. "What do you want?"

"Betsy Hannah?" asked the policeman.

"Yes, that's me."

"I'm Sergeant O'Connor and they are Lieutenants Miller and Kasinka. We understand that you are in a relationship with Nathan Nordstrom," he said.

Betsy hesitated for a moment before answering. Finally, she stammered, "We work together. We used to date, but not any longer. He's not here."

Sergeant O'Connor noticed the frightened look in Betsy's eyes and her nervousness. "Do you mind if we search the apartment? We do have a warrant," he said flashing her a formal looking document.

Betsy stepped aside and three officers with guns drawn entered her apartment.

"Are the guns necessary?" she asked as she continued to try to calm Maria, who was now crying hysterically.

Lieutenant Miller smiled at her. "Standard procedure," he said. "Is there anyone else in the apartment?"

"No, just the baby and me."

"You're not married?" he asked as he put his gun back into his holster.

Betsy stared at him in disbelief. "Please, tell me you are not hitting on me while you are in the process of ransacking my apartment."

He laughed and reached out to take Maria from her. "Here, let me try to calm her down. I have three nieces and two nephews, and I'm their number one baby sitter."

He gently bounced Maria up and down, and she instantly began to calm down. Within minutes, she had fallen to sleep with her tiny head nestled comfortably against his broad shoulder. "Where's her crib?" he whispered.

Betsy pointed toward Maria's room. Instantly, she remembered that she had left her phone lying on Maria's bed.

As Lieutenant Miller leaned over the crib, he noticed the phone. With one hand, he scooted it off to the side and laid Maria gently into the crib, tucking the blankets around her.

"Babies like to have their blankets tucked tightly around them." He then picked up the phone and handed it to Betsy. "Yours, I presume," he said.

"Thanks," said Betsy reaching for the phone and avoiding eye contact with him.

Sergeant O'Connor came to the door of Maria's bedroom. "If you're through playing babysitter, Lieutenant, we're ready to leave. Other than a couple of pictures of her and the suspect, there's no sign of him."

"Well, Miss Hannah. The next time you need help with your baby, let me know. I can be reached at Station B in the Village. Just ask for Jason."

Sergeant O'Connor slapped him on the shoulder. "Come on, Romeo. You're unbelievable." He then turned to Betsy. "If Mr. Nordstrom does get in contact with you, call us immediately. You could get yourself in a lot of trouble, if you don't," he said.

She looked down at Maria, and without looking up, she whispered. "He called me just as you came to my door."

She scrolled to the recent calls list and then handed her phone to Lieutenant Miller. "He told me to call him at the number listed there."

She heard him exhale deeply and saw him shake his head. "I didn't lie," she said quickly. "We are no longer in a relationship. I didn't intend to call him back."

"Sure, you didn't," said the Sergeant sarcastically. "Where is he?" he asked.

"He didn't tell me. You were knocking on the door just as he called. He knew it was probably the police. So, he told me to call him at that number, and then he hung up. Honestly, I don't know where he is."

"Call the number," said Sergeant O'Connor gruffly. "Find out where he is."

Betsy tapped on the number, and Nathan answered it immediately.

"It took you long enough to call me back," he said. "Who was at the door?"

Betsy sucked in a deep breath and looked at Lieutenant Miller. He looked away.

"It was the police," she said. "Nathan, where are you? Why don't you give yourself up? They'll find you, I'm sure."

"Not if I can get to Mexico. Unfortunately, my wallet was stolen, and I don't have any legal papers to show at the border. I need for you to go to my apartment and get my passport."

"Nathan, I can't do that. I just got Maria back to sleep. I am not going to help you if you truly tried to poison your aunt." She pushed the speaker button on the phone so the police could hear the rest of her call.

"She was going to die anyway. I just helped her along. I need her money to get out of another mess."

Sergeant O'Connor scribbled something on a notepad laying on the end table and held it up for here to see.

"OK. Nathan, I'll come. Tell me where you are."

"I'm in a little diner in the old warehouse area on Steele Avenue. Just pull in the parking lot and I'll come out."

The three policemen immediately left her apartment without looking back.

CHAPTER 22

Cody held on to Lauren's hand and gently massaged her limp fingers. He had not moved from her bedside for two days. He knew that every hour that she remained unconscious lessened her chances of recovery. Both she and the security guard had suffered severe concussions caused by their closeness to the point of the explosion and the probable impact of being thrown against the unforgiving brick wall or crashing head first onto the concrete floor of the warehouse. She also suffered a broken shoulder and minor cuts and burns.

Crystal lightly tapped on the door to Lauren's hospital room. "How's she doing today, Cody?" she whispered.

"Still the same," he muttered. "She hasn't shown any responsiveness to any stimulation we've tried."

Crystal reached out and patted his shoulder. "You look like hell," she said. "Why don't you go home and get some rest. I'll stay here with her and call you immediately if there is any change."

"No. I'm all right, honest. I've taken catnaps in this chair, and I have no intention of leaving her. I want to be the first person she sees when she wakes up."

Crystal didn't miss the positivity in his use of the word *when*, but from what she had heard from the neurologist treating Lauren and the sad news that the security guard had just passed away, she doubted the reality of its happening.

"Do you mind if I catch her up on the details of what's going on at the museum?"

"No, of course not. We need to talk to her, even if she doesn't respond. I'm sure she's probably wondering about all that anyway." He lifted Lauren's fingertips to his lips, kissed them again for the hundredth time, and then laid her hand gently down on the bed. He got up and offered Crystal his chair.

"Look," shouted Crystal. "She moved her hand. She must be trying to reach for you."

Cody immediately whipped around and grabbed Lauren's hand. He stared intently at her face. "Lauren," he whispered through his tears. "I'm here. I'm not leaving." He looked over at Crystal. "She squeezed my fingers. I felt it. It was weak, but it was definitely a squeeze."

"She's a fighter," said Crystal. "I know she can whip this."

A noise from behind them caused both of them to turn toward the door as Mrs. Livingston burst through it.

"Mom, what on earth are you doing here?" Cody couldn't believe his eyes. His mother hadn't been outside of the condo complex since she moved in there.

"My god, do something about that scraggly looking beard and comb your hair. You're a disgrace," said Mrs. Livingston. "I'm here because you and your doctor friends don't seem to be making any headway with waking up this girl."

"She's starting to come back," Cody defended. "She just squeezed my fingers."

"Well, whoopee ding dong," said Mrs. Livingston. "What she needs to do is open her eyes and talk to us."

Mrs. Livingston immediately shoved past Crystal to get a closer look at Lauren.

145

She certainly looks familiar, thought Crystal as she stared at the attractive, older woman. I wonder where I could have seen her before.

"I played a role once in which I was in a coma for days, but I woke up as good as new," said Mrs. Livingston.

Cody shook his head and let out an exasperated sigh. "Mom, please, that was in the movies for god's sake. Real life is a lot different."

"Hog wash. Haven't you ever heard that art imitates life? Of course, you have. I used to tell you that all the time. Anyway, what you moviegoers don't realize is that there is a lot of research that goes into making movies. The directors wouldn't have let me wake up after days of being in a coma if it weren't possible for me to do that. What Lauren has to do is to *will* herself awake."

"Mom, please, don't embarrass yourself with theatrics and wishful thinking," said Cody.

"I've never embarrassed myself in my life," said Mrs. Livingston. She marched over to the opposite side of Lauren's bed and leaned over close to whisper something in her ear.

To the amazement of Cody and Crystal, Lauren's eyelids fluttered and her lips parted as if she was about to speak.

"There," said Mrs. Livingston. "I told you so. Well, my work is done here. If you don't want to frighten her when she opens her eyes, you'd better do something about your disgusting appearance," she called over her shoulder as she left the room.

"Who is she?" asked Crystal. "I mean other than being your mother. She's really gorgeous for her age, and I have a feeling that I've seen her before."

"Lynette Starr," came a barely audible whisper from Lauren.

"Oh, my god. Crystal, did you hear that?" Cody leaned close to Lauren's face and kissed her lightly on the lips. "Lauren, please, open your eyes, please," he begged. "I love you and need you. Please, please, please open your eyes and look at me."

Tears streamed down Crystal's cheeks, and she reached up to flip them off her face. "I never cry," she muttered.

Cody stared intently at Lauren as her eyelids fluttered opened and closed several times before finally staying open.

"Hey, you," she whispered in a raspy voice. She reached up and touched his face with her uninjured hand. "Your mom's right; you do need a shave." She tried to raise her head to look over at Crystal but dropped back against the pillow. "Oh," she said closing her eyes again. "I have a terrible headache, and I'm really dizzy."

Cody laughed softly. "I'm sure you are. You've had a terrible blow to the head."

Crystal moved to the other side of the bed and leaned over it so Lauren could see her. "Hey, Lauren," she said smiling through her tears. "I'm sure glad to see you awake. I was afraid Betsy and I were going to have to finish the new exhibition by ourselves."

Lauren smiled. "You were the last voice I heard in that stinking, old warehouse. I heard you calling my name, but why were you there?"

"It's sort of a long story," answered Crystal. "Someday, I'll explain it all to you, but right now, all you need to know is that all the stolen art pieces are safely back in the Museum storage facility and Nathan and the other crooks will be spending a lifetime together in prison."

"Good," muttered Lauren as she closed her eyes again and drifted off to sleep.

"Lauren," called Crystal, but Lauren didn't respond.

Crystal glanced up at Cody. "Is she going to be OK? Why did she just fall back to sleep like that?"

"She's going to be fine. It's normal for her to come and go like that for the first several days. It's the body's way of helping her brain heal as the swelling goes down."

"I wonder what your mother said to her," said Crystal.

"I have no idea, but whatever it was, it must have been a jarring message to have reached Lauren's subconscious the way it did. Nothing my mother says or does ever surprises me. She's an amazing and horribly stubborn woman."

"My mother has an entire collection of her movies. We used to watch them together when I was a child. I thought she was dead," said Crystal.

Cody laughed aloud for the first time in two days. "Everyone thinks she is dead. But she was very young when she made her movies. She's more alive than most women half her age. She lives next door to Lauren."

"Oh, my gosh. She's Lauren's hateful neighbor? Lauren talks about her all the time. No way could Lynnette Starr be Lauren's nasty neighbor. Your mom was every woman's idol when my parents were growing up. My mother still has old movie magazines in her collection of memorabilia about your mother. I've read them. No one ever wrote anything but praise for her gentleness and kindness in life just as in the movies."

"Please don't let anyone know I told you where she lives. She's become a hermit and a terrible cynic. Unfortunately, life outside of the movies wasn't all that kind to her."

"But why would she come here to help Lauren? Lauren thinks your mom hates her."

Cody smiled. "She knows how hard I have fallen for Lauren, and believe it or not, she cares deeply for Lauren, too. Only her love for the two of us could have brought her here today."

CHAPTER 23

After two long weeks in the hospital, Lauren was glad to finally be home and going back to work. She walked out to her verandah to wait for Mary and Dan. She had missed their morning visits and the mental boost they always gave to her. The ocean was calm and the morning sky was even more beautiful than ever before. She inhaled deeply and slowly let the fresh air flow back out of her lungs.

"Good morning," called Mary as she came into sight. She was pushing a stroller and Rochester was following behind her. "It's so good to see you all dressed up and heading back to work."

"I see you're babysitting Maria. How's Rochester doing with her?"

Mary leaned over to pick up Rochester. "He's very protective of her and watches me like a hawk whenever I pick her up. By the way, I'm going to visit my pitiful nephew today. His trial starts pretty soon, and I want to add to his misery by telling him I've changed my will. To think that his greediness almost killed both of us." She clicked her tongue and shook her head. "Well, he didn't succeed. I'm grateful for that."

"Me, too," said Lauren.

"Enjoy this glorious day," called Mary as she leaned over and put Rochester back on the ground. "Come on, you lazy dog. If you're going to live long enough to enjoy part of my riches, you have to exercise more." She looked up and waved at Lauren as she continued to drag poor Rochester up the street behind the stroller.

Lauren smiled and shook her head. She still is going to leave some of her inheritance to that dog, but I'm betting the rest goes to her tiny second niece, Maria.

"Hey, you," called Dan as he came around the corner. "Good to see you up there again. I've been reading about you in the newspaper. He stopped the tricycle and took a bouquet of fresh flowers from a backpack strapped to the rear of his seat. "Here," he said, walking over to Lauren's verandah. "Catch."

Lauren leaned over to catch the flowers he tossed up to her. "Wow," she said. "I feel just like Juliet."

"Believe me, he's no Romeo," said a voice coming from Mrs. Livingston's verandah. "Hello, Daniel," she said.

Dan held his hand up to shade his eyes from the bright sun that had inched its way above the tiled roof of the condo building. He continued to stare up at Mrs. Livingston as he walked over to her verandah. "Oh, my god. Is that really you, Barbara?"

"You two know each other?" said Lauren.

"Can I come up there?" asked Dan directing his full attention to Mrs. Livingston and ignoring Lauren's question.

"You know you always had a double climb up to my balconies, so maybe you should park that ridiculous contraption you ride by here every day and come to the front door so I can buzz you in."

Lauren watched in astonishment as Dan grabbed his trike and threw it up on the sidewalk. She turned to face Mrs. Livingston. "What's going on here?" she asked.

"Don't you have someplace you're supposed to be?" replied Mrs. Livingston heading back inside her condo.

CHAPTER 24

"Well, I'm off. Big day ahead—Lauren's coming back today," said Crystal. "Here are your crutches but don't go getting all heroic and overdo your exercise today."

Jake reached up and pulled her into his lap. "I promise I'll be a good boy, but when you get back home tonight, we're going to make that phone call to your dad."

As she pushed herself up from the recliner, Crystal leaned over and kissed him. "I know, I know," she said.

"If you don't call him, he'll come out here—you know that. I think it'll be easier for you to tell him on the phone than in person."

Crystal glanced in the mirror that hung above the mantel in her apartment and straightened her hair. "I thought I might call my mom and let her tell him," she said.

Jake laughed. "Since when have you turned all chicken? Where's the brave woman who ran back into a burning building to save her friend?"

Crystal turned around to face him and smiled. "That was different, besides, unless I'm mistaken, you haven't turned in your notice either. So, where's the hero who broke rule number one to come and save me?"

"As always, you win. But, tonight we both make those calls, deal?"

"Deal," she agreed.

As she walked the short distance to the Museum, she felt both exhilarated and nervous. Was she making the right decision? All her life, the only thing she ever wanted to do was to follow in her father's footsteps, but now she wasn't sure.

The only thing that she was currently certain of was that she was in love with Jake and wanted desperately to start a new life with him here in California. For years, she had tried to deny her feelings for him, but when she thought that she might lose him at the warehouse, she knew she couldn't hide them any longer.

When he was released from the hospital, she had insisted that he come back to her apartment. The backs of his legs had been severely burned by the falling rafter and both legs had been broken in multiple places. But, thanks to skin grafts and modern medical practices that prevented infection, the doctors had told them that, with some physical therapy, he would soon be able to walk again without assistance.

As she approached the Museum, she saw Lauren walking toward her from the opposite direction. "Hey, you," she called. "Are you ready to start putting together the best exhibit this Museum has ever seen?"

"I am," said Lauren reaching out and hugging her around the shoulders.

"Then you won't fall apart when I break the bad news about the opening reception entertainment?"

"What?" said Lauren. "You've got to be kidding me."

"Nope. I wish I was, but the opening lecturer bailed— some illness in the family or something like that. So, it's up to us to come up with someone who will bring in the big donors, or else, to put it bluntly, we're screwed and so is the Museum."

Lauren suddenly stopped and turned to face her. "You know what? I just happen to know someone who I am sure will pack the house."

"Are you thinking about the same person that I think you are?"

Lauren laughed. "I am indeed."

"Good luck with that one," said Crystal. "And, to think that I thought calling my dad to tell him that I intend to stay on here as an associate curator was going to be a tough sale. You, however, are about to face the hardest sale of your young life."

"Seriously?" asked Lauren hugging Crystal. "You're really going to stay? I can't believe it. You certainly have made my day."

"Well, enjoy your euphoria while it lasts. The conversation that you are about to have with the reclusive Mrs. Livingston, aka, Lynette Starr, will most certainly bring an end to it."

Lauren slid her magnetic key across the reader and reached for the front door of the Museum. "We'll just have to see about that. I suspect that things are happening in Mrs. Livingston's condo right about now that may just bring her out of her hermitage."

"Surprise," shouted David Mesa and the rest of the Museum staff as she entered the open lobby. They were holding a big banner with 'We've Missed You,' printed in gigantic letters.

"See," said David. "Everyone came early just to welcome you back."

Lauren reached out to give him a hug. "I'm sorry about Josh," she whispered. "I know he was your friend. He actually kept me from getting hurt even more than I was.

154

He wrapped his arms around me right before the explosion. I think he knew what was about to happen."

David dropped his head. "He did good. I will miss him," he muttered.

CHAPTER 25

Lauren plopped down in a chair in her office and kicked off her stilettos. She was exhausted, yet relieved. The grand opening of the exhibit had been well received by the packed house of patrons and other invited guests. Even the weather had cooperated, and the dinner on the outside patio was perfect.

Cody tapped lightly on her door and stuck his head inside. "Can I interrupt your reverie?" he asked. "I just thought you might sneak up here to watch for the green flash."

Lauren smiled. "Guilty as charged," she said. "I am so glad this is over. Now I can actually start the job I came out here to do."

"It appeared that everything went off without a hitch tonight. Are you pleased with how it went?"

"I am," responded Lauren. "And, I can never thank your mother enough. She absolutely brought the house down. Everyone laughed themselves silly all the way through her monolog. She was amazing."

"I think you might have created a monster. She and Daniel are talking about going across the country on a tour. It's weird. I had no idea that he was living around here. He used to come to see her in LA after my dad left, but she finally drove him away like she did everyone else."

"As soon as you told me who he was, I remembered seeing him in her movies. He was always the friend who never got the girl," said Lauren.

"Well, I never expect to play his role," said Cody as he knelt down in front of Lauren. He reached in his pocket and pulled out a huge diamond ring. Taking her hand, he slipped it on her finger. "Will you marry me, Lauren Allen?"

Lauren threw both arms around his neck and passionately kissed him. "I will; I will. Of course I will," she shouted. "I love you. What a perfect ending to a perfect day."

"I love you, too," he said. He held her in his arms for several moments and then gently turned her around so they could watch the sun slip beneath the silky blue waters of the Pacific. "What a view," he whispered in her ear.

She leaned back against him and pulled his arms around her waist.

For several minutes, they just stood there staring out through the window—enjoying each other and another gorgeous California sunset. Suddenly, they both yelled, "There it is."

"I can't believe it. The elusive green flash is actually real," said Lauren.

"The green flash has always been real and is always there every time the sun sets or rises, but if you blink, you will miss it. My love for you is like that green flash—it happened in an instant, it is real, and it will always be there," whispered Cody.

She turned around to face him and reached up to hook both arms around his neck. "I have wonderful memories of people and things that I have seen from my windows, but tonight is the memory that I will cherish forever. I love you."

MARY LEE PECK

About The Author

Author, Mary Lee Peck, received her Ph.D. from The Ohio State University. She has been the author of both fiction and non-fiction books. Her passion for writing comes from her gift of storytelling. She admits that she likes a story with a happy ending. "Life can be frightening enough, so fictional reading should be a pleasurable experience—a way to escape from reality into a realm of make believe where the story ends the way it should," she asserts.

Her love for horses resulted in a series of books: *Raven's Call, Raven's Son*, and the soon to be released, *Raven's Return*.

Life in the small town where she spent the summers with her grandparents, inspired *The Mansion*, a story of a mansion that stands as an icon of love and commitment.

Breakfast with Friends is a mystery that discloses the horrors of human trafficking and the gumption of a motley group of friends ranging in age from 21 to 70. The friends have nothing in common but the diner where they meet for breakfast, but they ban together when one of the group is in trouble and come out on top against seemingly unbeatable odds.

The Family Bitch is a non-fiction book that describes human emotions that obstruct positive family relationships. The book contains real stories of women whose character has earned them the title of "The Family Bitch."

From my Window, takes place in a village in California where the author spends her winters. It is a mystery story about art theft that leads to romance between two individuals who have claimed they would never get involved in a romantic relationship again. From her window, Lauren Allen stares out at the ocean and seeks peace from her chaotic life, where no one seems to be who they claim to be.

www.ingramcontent.com/pod-product-compliance
Lightning Source LLC
Chambersburg PA
CBHW050951120626
46552CB00001B/491